Goddess Girls

PHEME
THE
GOSSIP

READ ALL THE BOOKS IN THE GODDESS GIRLS SERIES

Goddess Girls

PHEME
THE GOSSIP

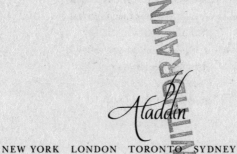

JOAN HOLUB & SUZANNE WILLIAMS

Aladdin

NEW YORK   LONDON   TORONTO   SYDNEY   NEW DELHI

This book is a work of fiction. Any references to historical events, real people, or real places are used fictiously. Other names, characters, places, and events are products of the authors' imagination, and any resemblance to actual events or places or persons, living or dead, is entirely coincidental.

ALADDIN

An imprint of Simon & Schuster Children's Publishing Division

1230 Avenue of the Americas, New York, NY 10020

First Aladdin paperback edition April 2013

Copyright © 2013 by Joan Holub and Suzanne Williams

All rights reserved, including the right of reproduction in whole or in part in any form.

ALADDIN is a trademark of Simon & Schuster, Inc., and related logo is a registered trademark of Simon & Schuster, Inc.

Also available in an Aladdin hardcover edition.

For information about special discounts for bulk purchases, please contact Simon & Schuster Special Sales at 1-866-506-1949 or business@simonandschuster.com.

The Simon & Schuster Speakers Bureau can bring authors to your live event. For more information or to book an event, contact the Simon & Schuster Speakers Bureau at 1-866-248-3049 or visit our website at www.simonspeakers.com.

Designed by Karin Paprocki

The text of this book was set in Berthold Handcut Regular.

Manufactured in the United States of America 0115 OFF

6 8 10 9 7 5

Library of Congress Control Number 2013930969

ISBN 978-1-4424-4937-4 (pbk)

ISBN 978-1-4424-6138-3 (hc)

ISBN 978-1-4424-4938-1 (eBook)

For Emily Williams and Jenny Lee Williams–
best ever daughter and daughter-in-law.
–S. W.

For Denise Prihoda Barbier, Jill Guidry,
Barbara Dupont Eppenger, Debbie King Mixon,
and Debi Sisley.
–J. H.

CONTENTS

1

Jackpot!

No ONE WAS AROUND AS PHEME SNEAKED down the hallway of the girls' dorm on the fourth floor of Mount Olympus Academy. She knocked on a door.

"Anybody home?" she called out softly.

As usual her words puffed from her orange-glossed lips. They rose above her head in little cloud-letters before floating away. Since she was the goddess of gossip and rumor, this was a useful gift. Any newsy tidbits she spoke when others were around were guaranteed to spread swiftly throughout the Academy.

Pheme waited a few seconds outside the door, listening for a reply. She wasn't surprised when she didn't get one. It was lunchtime. Most students were in the cafeteria. Perfect.

She turned the doorknob. It gave easily. Most girls at MOA didn't bother to lock their doors. Quietly she slipped into the room—Artemis's room. Along with Athena, Aphrodite, and Persephone, Artemis was one of the four most popular goddessgirls in the whole school. She was also one of a handful of girls who didn't have a roommate.

First thing, Pheme opened Artemis's closet. A mess as usual. Sports equipment and old school projects lay in a heap at the bottom. Rumpled chitons hung half on and half off the hangers. Artemis didn't care much about neatness or clothes. Of course, none of this surprised Pheme. She'd snooped in here before.

It was her job—sort of. Earlier in the year Principal Zeus had made her floor monitor for the girls' dorm. And that meant she was responsible for doing weekly safety checks.

Zeus had never been especially clear about *how* she was to carry out the checks. Or even what kind of hazards she should watch for. So she'd decided all that for herself. And her methods included room-snooping.

As she peeked into a random box inside the closet, her stomach growled with hunger. Normally she'd be at lunch too.

But today was Thursday. And although none of the other girls knew it, every Thursday she skipped lunch to make the rounds of their dorm rooms. To look for hazards. And if she came across some gossip-worthy information too—well, that was just the ambrosia frosting on the cake!

She fished out a snack bar from her chiton pocket, then munched on it as she began sorting through the stuff on the closet floor. Her hand brushed against a broken wooden arrow. Here was a *definite* safety hazard. You could get a sliver from the split shaft. Or cut yourself on the sharp arrow tip.

Pheme stuck the two halves of the broken arrow into the trash can by Artemis's desk. With all the mess in here, Artemis probably wouldn't even notice. She had no idea it was her turn for an inspection today. Next Thursday would be Athena and Pandora's turn.

Of course, it wasn't just physical objects—like broken arrows—that could pose safety hazards. Sometimes students *did* things that were dangerous. Like flying off to who knew where without first getting Zeus's permission. If Pheme uncovered such plans, it would be her duty to let Zeus know.

She smoothed out some crumpled papers she found in the trash and looked them over. Old math assignments. Nothing interesting. She tossed them in the trash again and headed back to the closet.

Today Pheme was really hoping to find more than broken arrows and other commonplace safety hazards. She needed to uncover some hugely hazardous information that Zeus absolutely needed to know. Something so mega-important that when she reported it to him, she'd win back his support and trust.

Because right now—just when she needed him to have confidence in her reporting abilities more than ever—Zeus had lost faith in her. Simply because she'd gotten it wrong about who'd stolen the Norse goddess Freya's necklace during the girls' recent Olympic Games. Honestly, anyone could have made that same mistake.

But try telling Principal Zeus that. He could be really unreasonable at times!

Pheme absentmindedly hung up a couple of Artemis's chitons before she realized what she was doing. Artemis would likely overlook a broken arrow in her trash. But for the most part things had to look undisturbed.

She threw the clothes back onto the floor. Then she tugged over a step stool and started digging around on the shelf above the clothing rod.

Regaining Zeus's support right away was critical. Until she could get back on his good side, he was unlikely to write her a glowing letter of recommendation. Which was something she needed to complete her application to *Teen Scrollazine*.

She just *had* to get the student staff reporter job that had opened up last week. Writing for *Teen Scrollazine* was her dream! Just imagine how it would impress her fellow students at MOA if she were in charge of covering important news stories. Finally she'd get some respect.

But she didn't have much time. She'd filled out the application days ago and was just waiting for the right moment to ask Zeus for a recommendation letter before sending it in. Both the letter and application were due on Monday, and—

"Whoa!" Something was staring at her from a dark corner of the shelf! Startled, she nearly fell off the stool. Was that a—a *head*? Wait. No. It was only an old Beautyology class project. The head form wore frightful makeup and a tangled wig.

Pheme remembered doing the same project back in fourth grade too. Only, as she recalled, her head form had turned out much better. Makeup and hair styling had never been Artemis's thing.

Owww-ooo-oo!

At the sound of howling out in the hall, Pheme froze. Dogs? There was only one girl in the MOA dorm that had dogs. Ye gods! Artemis was coming!

Panicking, Pheme kicked the stool away and leaped into the closet to hide. She made it only seconds before Artemis and her three hounds came into the room. The dogs made a beeline for the closet. She held her breath as they sniffed and scratched at the closet door. Were they after her, or the last half of her snack bar?

Her stomach growled again. Would Artemis hear?

Pheme wanted to jump for joy when she heard Artemis quickly bid her dogs farewell. "See you later, guys. I've gotta hit Principal Zeus's chariot safety lecture next period after lunch. And I can't have you chasing the chariots like last time. I promise we'll go for a run tonight after classes."

The door to the hall opened and closed again. And then Artemis was gone.

Phew! After waiting a minute Pheme popped out of the closet. The dogs jumped and wiggled, acting happy to see her. Not at all the reception *Artemis* would've given her if she'd caught her nosing around.

Most girls, Pheme knew, would likely disapprove of her room-snooping. If they ever found out, they'd probably get all mad and say she was taking her monitor job far too seriously. However, she got results! She'd uncovered and removed many safety hazards during her weekly dorm checks. Why, she'd probably even saved lives!

Still feeling a bit rattled from nearly being discovered, Pheme slipped out of the room. No way could she snoop effectively with those dogs hounding her the whole time.

No problem. She could finish going through Artemis's room next Thursday. Today she'd trade for Athena and Pandora's room instead. After moving farther down the hall, she paused outside their door. She called out to check that neither of them was inside. Then she carefully looked both ways. The coast was clear.

She darted inside, then closed the door soundlessly behind her. Her eyes scanned the room for anything of interest. Anything mega-hazardous that she could report. Unfortunately, everything seemed pretty much as usual.

As she passed Pandora's unmade bed, she noted the jumbled-up bedspread. The curious girl's pj's, which were covered with a pattern of question marks, lay in a heap on top of it. She and Artemis had messiness in common.

Athena's bed, by contrast, was neatly made. Her blue and yellow dotted bedspread hung evenly and without wrinkles.

Like in all the girls' dorm rooms at MOA, the beds were on either side of the room. (Artemis's dogs slept on *her* extra bed!) Beyond the beds were identical closets and built-in desks. The boys' rooms on the fifth floor were rumored to have the same setup. Pheme didn't know that for sure, because she'd never snooped in them. Except for the occasional party in the common room at the end of the boys' hall, girls weren't allowed up there.

If a rule was clearly stated like that, Pheme tried to follow it. She was nosy, but she wasn't a criminal! Before she'd begun room-snooping, she'd even checked the *Goddessgirl Guide*, to be sure there wasn't a rule against entering an empty, unlocked room. There wasn't. Probably because no one but her had ever thought of doing it!

Stopping by Pandora's desk, Pheme bent to examine an article from the *Greekly Weekly News* that was tacked to Pandora's bulletin board. POSEIDON WATER WAVES OPENS TO THE PUBLIC TODAY, read the headline.

The accompanying photo showed a cute godboy named Poseidon grinning big. He had designed the magnificent water park. Behind him you could see gracefully curving slides made of polished marble, gleaming fountains, and pools of turquoise water.

"Well, this is so not helpful, Pandora!" Pheme whispered to herself. "Update your bulletin board once a century, will you?"

The water park had opened way earlier in the year, just after Athena had first come to MOA. Back then Pandora had been crushing on Poseidon. But now she liked a Titan godboy named Epimetheus.

Not only was this article unworthy of reporting to Zeus, it was also old news. And nobody cared about old news. She needed *new* news!

Pheme moved on to Athena's side of the room. There was a tall stack of textscrolls piled neatly on her desk. Which could only be considered a safety hazard if they happened to topple over and fall on you, she thought wryly. Godness, that girl read a lot!

But that wasn't news. Pheme pictured herself announcing it in the cafeteria. *Guess what, everyone! Athena reads a lot!*

She could imagine the giant yawn that would spread over the entire room. Everyone would probably just take a nap. They already knew Athena was a brain and a half. The smartest girl at MOA, in fact. No, not news at all.

A surge of panic flowed through her as it always did

when she worried others might find her uninteresting. It was way more fun when they hung on her every word!

Glancing out the window, she noticed that the sundial read ten to one. Not much time left. "Come on, come on. There must be something exciting around here," she murmured.

Her brown eyes darted back to Athena's stack of scrolls. She scanned the titles. Besides the usual required class scrolls, there were several that Athena had checked out of the library, including *Invention and Innovation* and *A Concise History of Greek Inventors and Inventions That Changed the World*.

There was probably a whole chapter on Athena in the second scroll, thought Pheme. Athena had invented tons of useful things, including olive trees, flutes, farm plows, ships, and the modern chariot. *Principal Zeus must be very proud of his brainy daughter,* she thought wistfully.

Although he could be really stern and intimidating, Pheme totally respected him. And the praise he bestowed on her whenever she brought him a piece of particularly useful information was something that made her feel more . . . *worthy*. Growing up at home, she'd rarely gotten enough of that kind of positive attention.

Her gaze drifted over a pile of papers beside Athena's textscrolls. Several seemed to be sketches for new inventions. There were also scraps of papyrus with weird mathematical symbols and numbers scribbled on them. *Borrr-ing!*

Wait! What is this? Grinning, Pheme pulled out a notescroll with a row of *X*s and *O*s across the bottom. These were no mathematical scribblings. This was a note from Heracles, Athena's crush. How sweet!

Still—not news. And not a safety hazard, either. Starting to feel desperate, Pheme slid open Athena's desk drawer. Her entire face lit up when she saw what was inside.

Athena's diaryscroll! This was infinitely more interesting than any old safety hazard.

"Where have you been all my life?" Pheme asked it, giving the diaryscroll a quick kiss as she pulled it out.

She'd never run across it while snooping in here before. Athena must have been keeping it in a hiding place but forgotten to put it back. There wasn't even a magical locking ribbon tying it shut.

"How careless, Athena," she murmured in delight. "I'd think you'd be smarter than to overlook something like that. I mean, you're rooming with the most curious girl at MOA!"

Pheme slipped into Athena's chair and set the diaryscroll on the desktop, careful not to disturb anything else. Then she unrolled it little by little. Her sharp eyes searched eagerly for something juicy. Most of the entries were dull accounts of homework assignments needing to be done or homework already completed. Blah, blah, blah.

"Come on. Show me some good stuff," she said softly. "Something that Zeus would want me to report to him. Something that would make him write me the most mega-spectacular recommendation ever."

Snooping on Athena was a bit tricky. She was Zeus's daughter, after all. But if Pheme found out she was in trouble with her schoolwork or at odds with another student, he'd likely be grateful to know. However, since Athena was pretty much perfect, what were the chances of that?

"What are you doing!" a voice shouted.

Startled, Pheme leaped up, nearly having a heart attack. But then she relaxed, realizing she hadn't been discovered. The shout had come from outside.

She peeked out the window and saw that Hermes' silver-winged delivery chariot had touched down in the courtyard below. He'd only been scolding a student for getting in the way as he'd landed.

The back of his chariot was piled high with pack-ages, including some deliveries for MOA. She watched Hermes hop out and heft a load. When he started toward the Academy's front doors, Pheme caught a small move-ment among the packages he'd left behind in the chariot.

Was that a—a *hand* popping out? She blinked. When she looked again, it was gone. She squinted at the char-iot, long and hard, but the hand didn't reappear. She must have been seeing things, she thought, rubbing her eyes. And she was also wasting time. She plopped into Athena's chair again. Back to business.

She unrolled more of the diaryscroll. And then

gasped. Because almost immediately a word jumped out at her. It was her own name!

The entry was dated recently, during the girls' first Olympic Games. It read: *I'm so mad! Pheme told Dad that Aphrodite and Persephone stole Freya's necklace. Of course it was absolutely untrue.*

"Ye gods, cut me some slack, can't you?" Pheme whispered. Her cheeks burned anew with embarrassment. This was the very incident she was hoping to erase from everyone's minds—especially Zeus's—by reporting something else really big and newsworthy.

When Freya's fabulous jeweled necklace had disappeared during the Girls' Olympic Games, Pheme had glimpsed Aphrodite and Persephone holding something sparkly. Naturally she'd assumed it was the necklace. But it had turned out to be a jeweled collar for Adonis, the kitten they shared. Not Freya's necklace.

Hey, she didn't claim to be perfect. She was the goddess of gossip and rumor, not the goddess of thoroughly fact-checked information. Some people, Principal Zeus included, didn't seem to realize that gossip wasn't, and never would be, an exact science. It was more of an art, really. And she was a master at it—most of the time, anyway!

After the necklace incident Zeus had called her into his office and *ranted* at her. His disappointment in her had really hurt. She'd had to bite her lip to keep from crying.

She knew he valued her ability to uncover important information. That was the very reason he'd invited her to MOA years ago. She could still remember when her parents had given her the good news. For once she'd felt appreciated. Like she stood out. Being in a family of thirteen kids, it wasn't a feeling she was used to.

When Zeus had finally calmed down about the necklace, he'd said more gently, "You're my eyes and ears at MOA, Pheme. I depend on you for *quality* information. Do you understand? Information that will keep students out of trouble and safe from danger."

She'd nodded, but in truth it was hard to always figure out which pieces of information were worthy of his attention. What if she failed to report something he really needed to know? That could be disastrous! So she'd kept right on room-snooping. Just in case.

Pheme glanced down at the diaryscroll again. She was almost afraid to read any more, in case the words were hurtful ones. Turned out they kind of were.

I avoid Pheme as much as possible, Athena had written. *Honestly, that girl couldn't keep a secret if her life depended on it. Today she told Heracles that I said he treats his favorite knobby club like it's a beloved pet. And*

I did say that, but not to her. She must've overheard me.
She shouldn't go blabbing words said in private. What a
snoop! I mean, I wouldn't even put it past her to sneak into
my room and try to read you, diaryscroll!

Huh? Startled by the accuracy of Athena's words,
Pheme breathlessly unrolled more of the diary. She
read on.

Well, Pheme, if you or anyone else does read this, you'll
be sorry. Because I put a magic spell on it.

A magic spell? Pheme's eyes bugged out. She looked
around, wondering if there was a booby trap nearby
ready to spring.

She didn't see anything. But she did *feel* something.
Her fingertips were starting to tingle. They were turning pink! They went even pinker, before darkening to
red. Startled, she let go of the diaryscroll. It shut with a
snap, and she rammed it back into Athena's desk drawer.

Then she jumped up and just stood there staring at her hands in horror as the red spread. It zipped along her fingers, past her knuckles, and all the way up to her wrists, where it finally stopped.

Aghhh! Both of her hands looked like she'd dipped them in bright red paint. Athena's spell had worked.

Pheme had been caught *red-handed*!

2

Stowaway

FREAKING OUT, PHEME RAN FOR THE DOOR. SHE

forgot to look both ways as she left the room, but luckily

there was no one around. She scurried to the bathroom

at the end of the hall. Maybe the red stuff would wash off.

"Anyone in here?" she called out as she dashed inside

the bathroom. Her words puffed above her head. When

no one answered, she went straight to the sink. Using lots of soap, she scrubbed and scrubbed her hands. But no matter how hard she scrubbed, the red wouldn't come off.

Giving up, she stared at her pale, worried face in the mirror above the sink. She watched her reflection run red fingers through her short, spiky orange hair.

"What am I going to do?" she whispered aloud. She turned away from the mirror and glanced wildly around the room. There had to be a way to break Athena's spell. But how?

She paced, trying to remember the spells she'd learned in Spell-ology class over the years. None of them dealt with this exact situation. Still, maybe she could tweak one to make it work. Like that one for getting rid of pimples!

"Icky spots upon my face . . . uh . . . *fingers*," she began. Then, she remembered that the next line went: *With this spell all zits erase.*

She'd need to reword the spell carefully. After all, she didn't want to erase her *fingers*. Just the red. And she also needed a word that rhymed with "fingers." In a sudden burst of vocabularistic creativity, an idea came to her. She began again:

> *"Icky red stuff on my fingers—*
> *With this spell no trace of it lingers!"*

She glanced eagerly down at her hands and waited for her fingers to tingle like before. Then she'd know that the spell was beginning to take effect. But nothing happened. Her hands remained a bright cherry red. *Argh!*

Unable to think of another spell to try, Pheme considered other options. *How about gloves? No,* she decided. Wearing gloves would be weird and draw everyone's attention. And this was one time when she definitely didn't *want* attention!

Getting a sudden brainstorm, she dashed out of the bathroom and headed for the Beauty-ology classroom. The teacher, Ms. ThreeGraces, had all kinds of makeup in there. And more important—makeup removers. Maybe one of them would remove the red and undo this red-handed disaster.

Otherwise she didn't know how she was ever going to explain that she'd been snooping in someone's diaryscroll. A diaryscroll *was* pretty private. If Athena found out and told Zeus, she hated to even imagine his reaction.

At the very least he'd probably ask someone else to be

floor monitor and refuse to give her the recommenda-tion she needed for the *Teen Scrollazine* job. At the worst he might zap her with one of his thunderbolts!

Hiding her hands in the pockets of her chiton, Pheme hurried down the marble staircase. The Beauty-ology classroom was on the main floor of the Academy. Three floors down from the girls' dorm.

Just as she reached the bottom of the stairs, the cafe-teria doors opened across the hall. Out stepped the four most popular goddessgirls in the entire school. Golden-haired Aphrodite, green-eyed Persephone, arrow-packing Artemis—and diaryscroll-owning Athena.

Athena was pretty much the last person on all of Mount Olympus that Pheme wanted to see right now. What a nightmare!

The goddessgirls were laughing about something. Like Pheme, they were all immortals, so their skin

28

had a beautiful golden shimmer. (Mortal MOA students like Medusa and Pandora didn't have shimmery skin.) As soon as the four friends noticed Pheme, they clammed up. Guarded expressions stole across their faces.

Even though her hands were hidden, Pheme couldn't help worrying that Athena would somehow guess what she'd done. In fact, her cheeks were probably as red as her hands right now. From embarrassment and guilt!

Pheme tried to act normal. Only, she was nervous and couldn't think what to say. So she just stood there, staring bug-eyed at the girls.

They were starting to give her weird looks. Unfortunately, they were also unintentionally blocking her way down the hall to the Beauty-ology classroom. Abandoning her plan to go there for now, she turned and bolted out the bronze front doors of the Academy, then down the granite steps to the courtyard.

Taking long, deep breaths of fresh air, Pheme tried to calm down. Athena couldn't have guessed anything. The girl might be brainy, but she wasn't psychic!

Hermes' silver-winged chariot was still parked in the middle of the courtyard. Remembering the hand she'd seen—or *imagined* she'd seen—popping up from between packages, Pheme went over and peeked inside the back of the chariot.

It was empty. Which meant Hermes had already finished his MOA deliveries. He was probably hanging out with Principal Zeus in his office for a while before taking off again.

Hearing some godboys coming up from the sports fields, Pheme ducked behind the chariot. She didn't feel like talking to anyone right now.

With her back against the chariot, she sank down till

she was sitting on the courtyard's mosaic tiles. Her weight caused the chariot to roll forward a couple of inches, but then it stopped.

When the boys were safely past, she drew her hands from her pockets to examine them, hoping with all her heart that the spell had worn off. Nope. Still red. Her stomach sank. *Rats.*

"Hey! Thanks a lot!" a boy's voice complained from behind her. Startled, Pheme thrust her hands back inside her pockets. She glanced around worriedly. Had someone seen?

"Over here," the voice said. "Stuck, thanks to you."

Pheme whipped around. Sure enough, there was a boy lying on his back underneath the chariot behind her. She knew everyone at MOA, but she didn't recognize him. He looked about the same age as her, with sky-blue eyes and curly hair as golden as the sun.

"Who are you?" she asked.

"Whoa," said the boy, watching the puffy cloud-letters escaping her lips. "Awesome skill. I guess that means you must be a goddess, right?"

She nodded. Of course, her shimmery skin was a dead giveaway too.

"*Mega*-awesome! I've never met a goddess before!" He yanked on the hem of his tunic, which was wedged under one the chariot's wheels. It must've happened when the chariot had rolled forward.

"Um, sorry," she said as she watched him try and fail to wiggle the hem free. "Guess that's my fault. I'll help you. But turn your head away first. And don't look till I say so."

He shot her an odd glance but did as she asked. She took her hands out of her pockets and tried to push the wheel. It wouldn't budge.

32

"What's up with your hands?" he asked, having turned his head toward her again.

"I told you not to look!" she said, sticking them back into her pockets.

"Sorry," he said, pushing himself up onto his elbows. "I have trouble doing what I'm told sometimes." He gave her a cheeky grin.

"What are you doing here?" she demanded.

"Hiding," he said matter-of-factly. "I rode here in the back of Hermes' chariot. When he disappeared with a load of boxes, I jumped out. Then some nine-headed teacher came by, so I dove under here to hide."

"Ms. Hydra," Pheme informed him. "She's not a teacher. She's Principal Zeus's administrative assistant." Pheme worked for Ms. Hydra as an office helper one afternoon a week. Tons of stuff was always happening in the front office. It was pretty much the

33

perfect place for snooping on school business.

The boy gave the hem of his tunic a hard yank. There was a small ripping sound.

Pheme pulled her hands out again and grabbed the chariot wheel she'd leaned against earlier. "Stop. That isn't working. Help me rock the chariot instead."

"Okay," said the boy. "But hurry. Hermes is bound to be back soon."

As they both grasped the wheel, the wheels in Pheme's mind began to spin. "So you're a stowaway?" This was definitely news. Big news. Maybe it was exactly what she'd been looking for!

The boy shrugged as he tugged at the wheel. "Yeah, I guess so."

Just then the chariot finally budged, rolling backward a few inches. At the same time, they heard Hermes coming down MOA's front steps.

The boy slid out from under the chariot. "Yikes! I can't let Hermes see me. He'll tell my mom! And take me back home before I—" But then he cut himself off, like he was worried he'd said too much.

Pheme's eyes sharpened, and her gossip-gathering instincts went on high alert. But before she could get his name or find out anything else about him, the golden-haired boy scrambled to his feet.

"Bye, Red!" He gave her a cocky wave, then ran off downhill—away from the Academy.

She chased after him, determined to ask her questions. A few minutes later she stopped, panting. *Rats!* She'd lost him.

Hearing a flapping sound overhead, she looked up and saw Hermes' winged cart zoom off into the clouds. Well, that boy wasn't leaving MOA now that his ride was gone. If she kept an eye out for him, she'd find him sooner or later. And then she'd get some answers.

In the meantime she had other things to worry about. Like red hands. Stuffing them firmly inside her pockets, she turned back toward the Academy.

3
Red, Bright, and Eew!

By THE TIME PHEME REACHED THE COURTYARD, lunch had ended. There was still some time before fourth period, so students were trickling outside to enjoy the nice, sunny weather. They gathered in small groups near the flower boxes and statues set here and there. Or on the granite steps or marble benches rimming the courtyard.

As Pheme started up the steps, she passed some girls sitting together and chatting. One of them, a goddess with rainbow-colored eye shadow named Iris, stopped speaking and eyed her warily. When Pheme returned her stare, Iris casually looked away.

How disappointing! In Pheme's experience the students who *didn't* look away were often the ones with the good gossip. They usually waved her over, wanting her to spread news that would benefit them somehow. Stuff that would make them more popular at MOA or more famous down on Earth.

Of course, sometimes those who avoided her gaze turned out to have good gossip or secrets too. Figuring all of this out was almost a full-time job. And Pheme was great at it!

Hearing a familiar laugh, she froze halfway up the

steps. Above her Athena and her friends were on their way down. *Great. Just great.*

As usual the four goddessgirls were laughing, looking like they were having fun. It always seemed to her that they didn't have any problems. But she knew that wasn't true. Because every now and then she discovered that one of them did have a problem. And since she was the goddessgirl of gossip, she usually couldn't help telling the world about it!

When Athena glanced at her, it was Pheme who looked away this time. Hoping she didn't look too guilty, Pheme rushed on past.

For one awful second she suddenly wondered if she'd remembered to straighten the stuff on Athena's desk before leaving her dorm room. She was usually so careful about things like that. But she'd been frantic. Inside her pockets she crossed her red fingers that if she *had* forgotten, Athena wouldn't notice.

Near the top of the steps Pheme saw Pandora. Her blue-streaked golden hair made her kind of hard to miss. She was asking questions of a couple of girls who seemed to be trying to ditch her.

One of them noticed Pheme and pointed her out to Pandora, saying, "Oh, look. I think Pheme wants to talk to you." When Pandora glanced over at Pheme, the girls darted away.

Oblivious to the snub, Pandora flashed Pheme a genuine smile and waved. Pandora never seemed to mind Pheme's gossipy nature and didn't try to use her to spread gossip either. Maybe that was because she was as curious as Pheme was nosy, so they had a lot in common. The two of them, ignored by many students, had become friends.

"Where've you been?" Pandora asked when Pheme caught up to her. She brushed back the question-mark-shaped bangs that were plastered to her forehead. "I saved you a seat at lunch, but you didn't show."

Pheme hesitated. She couldn't very well tell Pandora the truth—that she'd been snooping in Athena's and her room. "I wasn't hungry," she said smoothly. As if on cue, her stomach rumbled loudly. *"Then,"* she added to the words that had already puffed above her head.

"Want this?" Pandora drew an apple from her pocket and held it out. "I was going to save it for later, but I can get another one."

Pheme automatically started to reach for the apple. In the nick of time she caught herself. She shoved her red hands deeper inside her pockets.

"No, thanks. You keep it," she told Pandora. "I'll grab something from the snacks table in the cafeteria. Ta-ta!"

She angled her head and smiled a good-bye. After all, she couldn't very well wave!

At the top of the steps, Pheme paused uncertainly in front of the Academy's bronze doors. She stared at the big golden door handles. *Uh-oh.* How was she going to open them without anyone seeing her hands?

Turning sideways to the door, she reached out one hand, still keeping it tucked inside her pocket. The fabric of her chiton *stre-e-etched* as she tried to grab the handle. *Rats.* It wasn't enough. She was going to rip her chiton if she forced it any more.

She was about to take a chance and pull her hands from her pockets, when a group of godboys—Ares, Apollo, Poseidon, and Eros—came up behind her.

"Going in, or staying out?" asked Poseidon. Impatiently he tapped the end of his trident, a three-pronged spear, against the top step. "C'mon. We've got to drop off some stuff before we head to the gym for the chariot safety lecture."

Pheme jumped a little as water droplets sprayed from the trident. She wanted to wipe them off her arm, but didn't dare. At one time Pandora and Medusa had both had crushes on this handsome turquoise-skinned godboy of the sea. But Pheme just thought he was a drip.

"I . . . uh . . . ," she stuttered.

Before Pheme could say anything more, Ares spoke up. His face was full of pretend amazement. "Pheme? Speechless? This is a first," he cracked.

"I'm going in, I guess," she said quickly.

"Well, don't hurry on our account," Apollo teased when she still didn't budge. The dark-haired godboy of truth, prophecy, and music was Artemis's twin. His band, Heavens Above, played for all the school dances.

Ares was Aphrodite's crush. But despite his blond hair and muscles, Pheme had never really understood what Aphrodite saw in him. Because sometimes he could be a bit tough. A bully almost. Of course, he was the godboy of war, so that went with the territory. And being around Aphrodite seemed to soften his hard edges some. So maybe they did make a good pair.

The boys had all laughed at Ares' "joke."

All except Eros, that is. "Never mind them," he said now. His glittery gold wings fluttered gently at his back as he stepped toward the door.

Pheme studied his wings while he reached for the door handle. Very few students possessed wings. They were so cool. And speedy.

You could move pretty fast with the magic winged sandals available to all students at MOA, but real wings were even better. If she had a pair, she could spread gossip way faster than she could now.

Eros shifted the bow and quiver he carried over one shoulder. Then he pulled open the door and held it for her. Her eyes darted away from his wings. She hoped he hadn't noticed her staring.

"After you, m'lady." He waved an arm wide and held his friends back so she could go in first.

Pheme liked his apple-red cheeks and the mischievous twinkle in his chocolate-brown eyes. They made him look happy. She could never decide if he was cute or handsome. But he was definitely gallant. And fun. That's probably why he had lots of friends.

"Thanks," she told him. With her head held high—and her hands safely inside her pockets—she stepped through the doorway.

"Cool doodles in class today," he said as she passed him.

"Huh?" she asked, surprised when he followed her.

"In Hero-ology. I saw your notescroll."

"Oh, yeah." She was a little hyper sometimes and doodled all over her notescrolls. A habit of hers when she was thinking. "Well, see you." She sped up, heading for the Beauty-ology room. She was on an un-red-handing mission. The last thing she needed was him and his friends hanging around her right now!

"Did you shoot yourself in the foot with your own arrow or something?" she heard Apollo tease Eros behind her. The other boys laughed.

"Wouldn't be the first time," Eros said good-naturedly.

What was that about? she wondered.

Because Eros was the godboy of love, his arrows had

a special power. Whoever they pierced fell immediately in love with the next person they saw. It was kind of a dangerous gift, in her opinion. If Eros made a mistake, people who didn't like each other one bit could suddenly think they were in love!

Did Apollo mean he thought Eros liked her? Pheme considered that weirdly new idea as she hurried down the hall. *Hmm.* Eros *had* chosen her to accompany him down the aisle in Principal Zeus and Hera's wedding. They'd been one of seven bridesmaid and groomsman pairs. And ever since the wedding Eros seemed to go out of his way to be nice to her. But he was nice to everyone.

The idea that he could be crushing on her was dumb, she decided. It wasn't like he'd purposely selected her to be a bridesmaid. It was just that she'd won his contest. Her name, written on a slip of paper, had been one among dozens tacked to a target Eros had set up. When all was ready, he'd taken aim and shot an arrow from fifty paces.

It had been pure luck that his arrow had pierced the slip with her name.

Hadn't it?

4
Secrets

HELLO? MS. THREEGRACES?" PHEME CALLED

out cautiously as she entered the Beauty-ology room. No

reply.

By now fourth period had started. Everyone was at

the chariot safety lecture in the gym, which she was

perfectly happy to miss out on. She'd attended enough

of them over the years. Lots of chariots racing around a track while Principal Zeus issued dire warnings and cautions. No, thank you!

Pheme made a beeline for the shelves at the back of the classroom. All the cosmetics were lined up on them in neat groupings according to use. There were bottles of nail polish that could magically change colors, for example, and eye shadows that could make your eyes appear a different color.

But she wasn't interested in those. Instead she went straight for the shelf of Un-Spellers. These were magical lotions that erased magic-made beauty mistakes. Like if you magically dyed your eyebrows purple by accident, you could use an Un-Speller to get out the dye.

She grabbed a tube of Super-Duper-Mega-Strength

Un-Speller, hoping it would take away the red. After glopping some onto her palms, she smoothed it over both her hands. Then she waited for the tingle. And waited.

Argh! Nothing happened. The power of Athena's spell was apparently even stronger than Super-Duper-Mega-Strength Un-Speller! This was bad. Very bad.

It meant that this red-handed spell could only be overcome by a much stronger spell. Figuring out the perfect Overcoming Spell would mean studying her Spell-ology scroll for hours and would take lots of trial and error.

"I do *not* have time for this!" Pheme huffed. Quickly she sorted through some little pots of concealer, hoping to find a temporary fix. "Yes!" she exclaimed when she found one that matched her fair complexion.

FOREVER FAIR said the label on the box in swirly letters. Beneath that were the words: *"Caution: Magic concealer lasts through time, but not through washing. Do not add water."*

"No hand washing. Got it," she said to herself.

Since she wouldn't be able to wash her hands after she applied the concealer, she used the sink in a corner of the room to wash them now. A few minutes later she was standing before a makeup mirror, ready to begin.

Scritch-scratch. Scritch-scratch.

Pheme looked around nervously. "Who's there?"

Suddenly the lid popped off a small round box sitting on the next table over. Out flew a magic makeup brush. Eager to help, the brush zoomed up to Pheme and hovered just inches in front of her face. So close that she went cross-eyed for a minute.

She backed up and grinned. "Yes, okay. I see you. And of course you can help."

At her invitation the brush gleefully swooped down to the pot of concealer and dipped into it. Then it darted straight for her nose.

"No!" She ducked away. "Not my face. These!" She held her hands up and wiggled her fingers in front of the brush. "I need to cover up the red."

The brush reared back as if shocked by the sight. Recovering quickly, though, it got busy whisking the magic concealer on until only Pheme's fingernails remained red.

After examining her hands, she said, "Perfect! Now it just looks like I have red nail polish on." She gave the makeup brush a thumbs-up. "Thanks!"

The brush curved its bristle tips toward her, executing a little bow. Then it did a dozen back flips to land in its box again. The lid shut tight after it.

What did it do in there when it wasn't helping out, she wondered? If only it could actually talk, it would be fun to interview it for *Teen Scrollazine* once she got the reporter job. Imagine the stories it could tell—about who had zits and who had used it to cover up a wart or whatever. She'd love to know everyone's makeup secrets!

Pheme snatched up the pot of concealer to return it to the shelf, then tucked it into her pocket instead. She might need a touch-up if the concealer somehow accidentally washed off.

Just as she hurried out the classroom door, Ms. ThreeGraces came around the corner. The teacher was impeccably groomed as always. Luckily, she was busy talking to a couple of girls with long, straight hair about a seriously hairy problem—split ends. None of them even noticed Pheme as she stole down the hall.

Her fifth-period class was Revenge-ology with Ms. Nemesis. The classroom was at the end of another hallway, but class wouldn't start for a while. Since the cafeteria was on the way, Pheme ducked in for a snack. By now she was starving!

The cafeteria was deserted except for a few lunch ladies at the far side. As the goddessgirl of gossip, Pheme's hearing was exceptionally good. So even from clear across the room she was able to hear them saying: "Ambrosia surprise? Nectar à la mode?" New menu ideas, she guessed.

She wandered over to the snacks table and grabbed a little box of raisins. She gobbled them down, then checked her hands. Awesome! None of the concealer had rubbed off so far!

Smiling, she rummaged through the snacks for a bag

of ambrosia chips. There weren't any, but sometimes extras were stored in the cupboard beneath the snacks table. It was something not many students knew, but Pheme had discovered it while snooping one day.

Bending down, she opened the cupboard. A boy tumbled out! The golden-haired boy from Hermes' chariot! His mouth was stuffed full, and he had a half-eaten bag of chips in his hands. Caught by surprise, crumbs sprayed out of his mouth.

Then he recognized her and calmed down. "Hey, Red!" he said, jumping to his feet.

"Stop calling me that!" she hissed, snatching a bag of chips from the cupboard. She glanced over at the lunch ladies, wondering if she should turn this boy in.

Spotting one lunch lady with a long snout like an anteater's, Pheme got distracted for a few seconds, watching her nose around the floor and countertops.

What is that lady doing? she wondered. *Sucking up crumbs? Ick!*

When she turned back to the boy, she found him staring at her hands. Self-conscious, she put them behind her back.

"How come just your fingernails are red now?" he asked, stuffing a few more chips into his mouth.

"Shh," she cautioned him, nodding toward the lunch ladies.

"They aren't listening," he told her.

He was right. The lunch ladies didn't appear to be paying any attention to them.

"Yeah, but they'll be able to read anything I say." She pointed to the words puffing over her head as she spoke. To be on the safe side, Pheme grabbed his arm and towed him over behind the tray return. They'd be partially hidden there.

"Okay, spill it," she told him, plopping down on a random chair. "What are you up to? Why'd you come here? I don't even know your name!" She ripped her chips open and began munching.

The boy sat too, propping his feet in another chair. "I don't know yours either, unless it really is Red."

Pheme was a little annoyed that he didn't recognize her as the goddess of gossip. But then she was only a *minor* goddess. She wasn't anywhere near as well known as Athena and her friends. All that would change once she got the job as a reporter for *Teen Scrollazine*, though. Mortals and immortals alike read it. She'd soon make a name for herself in print!

In the meantime maybe it was best that he *didn't* know who she was, since she wanted to ask him more questions. If he realized who she was, he might clam up.

"Okay, no names for now," she said. "We'll go by

58

nicknames instead. You can call me Red if you want to." She glanced at his hair. "And I'll call you Goldie. But, still, you have to answer my other questions."

"Sure," he said agreeably. "You already probably figured out I'm from Earth, right?"

She nodded encouragingly, which always got people to continue. Usually they had stories bursting to get out, and it didn't take much to get them going.

"Well, on the way to school down on Earth this morning, I saw Hermes' chariot parked on the street." He paused, his eyes sparkling. "It's awesome, don't you think? Those silver wings." He sighed rapturously. "Most chariots are pulled by horses, but—"

Pheme swallowed a chip, then interrupted. "All right. I get it. You're obsessed with chariots. Could you get to the point, though?"

The boy grinned. "Yeah. Sorry. My mom says not

everyone finds chariots as fascinating as I do."

Pheme tossed another chip into her mouth. "Um-hum. Go on," she mumble-crunched.

"Anyway," he said, "when I saw Hermes' chariot just sitting there, with him not in it, this irresistible urge came over me. I wanted to see what it was like to sit in the driver's seat. So I climbed on up. And then I couldn't resist tinkering with the controls. But just as I got the wings to flap, I heard Hermes coming back."

"Ye gods," said Pheme, her eyes going wide. People could be touchy about their chariots, especially Hermes. Artemis too, come to think of it. Aphrodite had a cart drawn by swans, but Artemis was the only student at MOA with a real, actual chariot kept on the school grounds.

Goldie nodded. "Exactly. So I dove into the pile of packages in the chariot."

"And became a stowaway," Pheme guessed.

"Only accidentally," he told her. "I didn't mean to end up at MOA. But now that I've had a look around, I think I'd like to go to school here, instead of down on Earth. Your school is way better than mine, with tons more interesting-sounding classes." He smiled and popped an ambrosia chip into his mouth. "Better snacks, too. These chips are to die for."

"Think so?" said Pheme. "If you really want something to die for, just let Zeus find out you came here uninvited." She drew a finger across her throat and made a choking face. "Believe me, you don't want to put him in a bad mood. And anyway, ambrosia chips *aren't* to die for. Ambrosia and nectar are what make immortals' skin shimmer."

"Yeah, I know," said Goldie. "We're not totally clueless down on Earth. We study Immortal-ology at my school." He cocked his head at her. "Hey, what are you the goddess of anyway?"

"The goddess of telling Zeus about you if you don't give me a good reason not to," she warned. She hoped her statement would distract him from his question about her identity, and it did.

"Great!" he said, surprising her. "Once I tell him who I am, I bet he'll invite me to go here." He leaped to his feet, looking enthusiastic. "So, what are we waiting for? Let's go see him."

Actually, news of a stowaway was exactly the kind of thing Zeus would expect her to bring to him. But Pheme wanted to have her facts straight this time before she did. Facts like this mortal boy's name and what he was up to. Her instincts told her there was more to his tale than he'd yet told her.

"Zeus is a busy guy. I can't just take any old stranger to

his office," said Pheme. Then she paused, waiting.

"I'm not just any old stranger. My dad's a god," the stowaway said in a cocky voice.

Stunned, Pheme stared at him. Now, this was unexpected news! Her mind raced ahead. If it was true, this could turn out to be an even bigger story than she'd first imagined. One sure to get Zeus's attention. In a *positive* way.

If they went to his office now, though, Zeus might get all blustery like he sometimes did when rules were broken. And he might just send Goldie home before she could get all the details of whatever mischief he could be plotting!

Still, it was hard for her not to go to Zeus right away. For once she was back on his good side, it would be a snap to get him to write that letter of recommendation she needed. At least she hoped so. The application was due in just four days, counting today.

"Really?" she said, struggling to contain her excitement. "Which god is your dad?"

Goldie shot her an uncertain look. "I'm not supposed to say. It's kind of a secret."

Pheme sighed in frustration. Honestly! No one at MOA, Zeus included, had any idea how hard she worked. Aphrodite only had to stand there and look beautiful and give others a few beauty tips now and then to be a success. Athena was naturally brainy, which made schoolwork easy for her. Artemis was a crack shot at archery and seemingly unafraid of anything. And Persephone was born with an incredible magic touch with flowers. She had the green thumbs to make *any-thing* grow.

They all had it made, in Pheme's opinion. But on top of her schoolwork and helping Ms. Hydra in the office, Pheme also had a full load of snooping and dorm monitor duties to do to fulfill her role as goddess of gossip and rumor. She was just lucky that snooping was something she enjoyed.

Seeming to sense her impatience, the boy offered more. "I guess it's okay to tell you my name. It's Phaeton." (Which he pronounced FAY-eh-ton.) "Since my dad's a god, I figure that also makes *me* a god, right?"

Pheme sent him a skeptical look. "Your skin doesn't shimmer."

"Yeah, I know. See, in my family, parents have to pass on a special mark of immortality. Like some kind of tattoo or something. I don't really know what it is," he admitted. "My mom separated from my dad when I was a baby, and she doesn't talk much about him. But he is a god. An important one."

Pheme shrugged. "If you say so."

"I'm not lying. My mom told me he was," he said, frowning. "It's true!"

She studied her red fingernails, as if she'd suddenly lost interest in their conversation. It was a strategy that often made people cough up information they'd previously been reluctant to share. Would it work this time? She held her breath, hoping.

"If I say who my dad is, do you promise you won't tell anybody?" he asked finally.

Pheme squirmed, wanting to jump for joy. She didn't want to appear too eager, though, and she also didn't want to make a promise she knew she wouldn't be able to keep. Instead she simply twisted her thumb and index finger together at the corner of her lips, as if turning a key to lock them shut.

"Tell you what," she said. "If you say who your dad is,

I'll try to get you enrolled at MOA like you want."

She was careful not to actually promise she wouldn't tell his secret. Would he notice?

And she'd only said she'd *try* to help him to go to MOA. She hadn't said how *long* he'd be able to stay after she helped enroll him. It might only be till Zeus sent him back with Hermes on his next delivery!

Luckily, Phaeton seemed satisfied. Grinning, he held up a hand, and they high-fived. "Deal!"

5
Phaeton's Dad

"So? WHO'S YOUR DAD?" PHEME LEANED TOWARD

Phaeton, waiting.

"Not so fast." Phaeton folded his arms, looking stubborn. "Convince Principal Zeus to let me into the Academy first. Then I'll tell you."

"But—," Pheme protested.

Just then the anteater lunch lady came sniffing

around. "Shoo, you two!" she told them. "I'm tracking down an ant infestation." She stuck her long snout behind the tray return. Her eyes narrowed. Then came that sucking sound again.

"Gotcha!" the lunch lady said gleefully.

Pheme made a face. *Blech!*

"All right," she told Phaeton as they left their hideaway. "You win."

His expression brightened. "So we'll go see Zeus right away?"

"No!" she said. "We can't let *anyone* see you till we're ready."

"I'm ready now," Phaeton said with a frown. "Can't we just go ask him?"

"That depends. Do you like being struck by thunderbolts?" she asked.

"He wouldn't do that," Phaeton scoffed.

"Well, okay, that was a bit of an exaggeration. But he hates being told what to do. He definitely might zap us a little if we just go in there and insist that he enroll you. Don't worry, though. I've got a plan."

Pausing at the cafeteria exit, Pheme reached up to wave her cloud-words away as soon as she spoke them. Just in case the lunch ladies were looking.

Then she turned to Phaeton and said, "Now hold still. I'm going to cast a spell over you." Before he could protest, she began to chant:

"Hide this boy from every gaze.
Invisible make sure he stays."

"C'mon," she told him then, pushing through the cafeteria doors.

"Did you really just make me invisible?" he asked, following her.

"Yep."

"Then how come it seems like you're still looking right at me?"

"Because you're invisible to everyone *except* me," Pheme replied. "But if you get more than ten feet away from me, you'll automatically turn visible again. So don't wander off."

When she started down the main hall, Phaeton stuck close, as ordered. She'd only recently perfected her invisibility spell. Good thing too, she thought as they began to climb the marble staircase to the upper floors. She was breaking all sorts of rules by skipping class and smuggling Phaeton upstairs. Boys weren't supposed to go on the girls' floor at all!

They passed a godboy with a lizardlike tail who was heading downstairs. "Hey, who's doing that? Stop it!" he suddenly yelped.

Huh? Pheme glanced behind her just in time to see Phaeton lift his foot off the godboy's tail.

"Oops! Sorry," she told the lizard boy quickly, pretending she'd been the one who'd stepped on his tail.

The godboy only grunted and continued down the stairs. He was in her Revenge-ology class next period. Which reminded her that she was going to miss class. Which meant she would have to come up with an excuse for skipping to give Ms. Nemesis tomorrow.

Maybe she could say that her absence had been a health issue? Because she'd absolutely *die* if she didn't find out who Phaeton's dad was! Okay, not really, *really* die. Immortals couldn't die, after all. But finding out did feel like a matter of life and death to her right now.

"Behave!" Pheme told Phaeton as they kept climbing. "Or else. I do know other spells, you know. Like how to turn an annoying boy into a frog."

As she waved away her cloud-words, he gave her one of his cheeky grins. "Okay, okay. I just wanted to see if I was weightless as well as invisible," he said. "Guess not."

Pheme rolled her eyes, thinking, *Good guess.* She didn't say it, though, because a couple of students were up ahead. She didn't want them to see her puffed words and think she was talking to herself!

Finally they reached the fourth floor, and she led Phaeton to her room at the end of the hall. When she'd first come to MOA, she'd roomed with Medusa. But Medusa had developed a mysterious allergy to the cloud-words Pheme spoke. So Pheme had moved out.

Oddly enough, she and Medusa had started hanging

out together soon after that. And Pheme's puffed cloud-words didn't seem to be a problem anymore. Weird. It was like Medusa's allergy had completely disappeared once she'd gotten her way and had a room to herself.

When they reached her room, Pheme opened the door and ushered Phaeton inside. "Wow. You're neat," he said, having a look around.

"Thanks," she said, taking that as a compliment. Because Medusa had more or less booted her out, Pheme was among the handful of girls at MOA without roommates. She liked keeping her room orderly. Still, it wasn't as tidy as Aphrodite's. That girl was a major neat freak!

However, Pheme's wasn't full of heart-shaped pillows. Instead she'd jazzed things up in her own personal style. She'd bought bold-colored orange and lime-green bedspreads with a geometric design, for example. And she'd hung a cool beaded curtain over the window.

She'd also hung a dozen orange-framed pictures on the wall above her bed. "Who are all these people?" Phaeton asked, studying one of them. "That's you in the middle, isn't it?"

He was staring at a drawing of her family—thirteen kids plus two parents. She'd sketched it herself the week before she'd left home to come to MOA.

"Yep, I was a smack-dab-in-the-middle child." She loved her big family, but she had *not* loved being overlooked and ignored. That's how it had felt to her, at least.

She'd thought things would improve when Zeus had invited her to come to MOA. But among so many amazing immortals, she still didn't stand out. For instance, even with the clue of her cloud-puffed speech, Phaeton hadn't been able to guess which goddess she was.

Well, all that was going to change. When she was a *Teen Scrollazine* reporter, her name would be right there under the titles of all the important news stories she wrote. She'd be famous and probably travel to exciting places to cover breaking news and meet kings and queens and stuff. Awesome!

When she opened the doors to her spare closet, Phaeton came to look over her shoulder. "Where'd you get all this stuff? What are these? Office supplies?" He reached into the closet and tugged at a random file.

"Stop that!" she said, waving him away. "Those are private." Honestly, this boy was almost as snoopy as she was!

On the third shelf down there was a stack of MOA forms. Pheme bent to sort through them. Since she had two closets and only needed one for clothes, she'd fitted this extra closet with shelves and turned it into a supply cupboard. This was also where she stored her "snoop" files—alphabetized folders full of newsy tidbits she kept on everyone.

"The supplies and stuff are from the front office, if you must know. I help Zeus's assistant, Ms. Hydra, in there on Wednesdays. Sometimes she gives me supplies she doesn't need anymore. And I also fish all kinds of interesting forms and junk from the wastebasket when she isn't looking. Which is not exactly easy, since she's got nine heads. That's eighteen eyes that could catch me at it."

"Why risk it?" asked Phaeton.

"Because you never know when something might come in handy. Like now, for instance. Bingo!" Pheme plucked out the form she'd been searching for. It was an official student enrollment form, a used one that Ms.

Hydra had tossed into the trash when this particular student had left MOA.

After shutting the closet she went and sat down at her desk with the form. She pushed aside some homework she'd completed the night before, then grabbed her favorite orange feather pen and her special magic eraser. She gave the eraser instructions:

> *"Take this form and please erase.*
> *Then write like Ms. Hydra in each space."*

Eager to get to work, the bespelled eraser immediately attacked the homework she'd pushed aside.

"No!" she yelled, diving for the papyrus sheets just in time to save her hard work from being undone. "That's my homework. It doesn't need erasing." She pointed to the form. "That form does."

"Wow! Where'd you get that thing? It is *sooo* awesome!" said Phaeton as the eraser got to work.

"From a store called Pentastic in the Immortal Marketplace," she told him.

When the eraser had finished its job, she picked up the pen. She filled in the first line, and the pen dutifully made her writing look like Ms. Hydra's, as instructed.

"No. With a *P-H*, not an *F*," Phaeton corrected when he saw how she'd written his name.

Pheme erased again and started over. "Maybe you'd better help me," she suggested.

Phaeton dragged over the chair from the other desk. Then he sat by her and nodded toward the form. "What's this for, anyway?" he asked.

Raising and lowering her brows in a mischievous way, she tapped the enrollment form with the feather end of her pen. "It's your ticket into MOA. At least it will be after we finish filling it out. Now, what's the name of your old school on Earth?"

"Why do you need to know that?" Phaeton asked.

"The form wants to know. Not me," she told him. "Just answer."

"Okay," Phaeton said reluctantly. "First word is *I-M-A*. Second word, *L-U-Z-E-R*. Then, 'Middle School.'"

Pheme wrote the four-word school name. Rereading what she'd written, a giggle escaped her. "Ima Luzer Middle School?" She glanced over at Phaeton.

He sighed. "I know, I know. It sounds like 'I'm a Loser Middle School.' Ha. Ha. Ha. That's just one more reason I'd rather go to MOA."

"Understandable," Pheme sympathized. As she added class and locker assignments, her pen continued imitating Ms. Hydra's handwriting.

"Who'll I be rooming with?" Phaeton asked when

they came to the dorm room assignment line.

"How about Heracles?"

His face lit up. "Are you serious? The mortal hero Heracles, you mean? The one with the awesome club weapon?"

Pheme nodded. She'd remembered Athena mentioning once that Heracles didn't have a roommate. Well, he did now! Quickly she went to her closet and fished out the room assignment list she'd copied from Ms. Hydra's desk. Finding Heracles' room number, she wrote it in the required blank.

"All done!" she announced once all the blanks had been filled in. After rolling up the faked enrollment form, Pheme grabbed the latest issue of *Teen Scrollazine* from a shelf above her desk.

"Now what?" asked Phaeton.

"Now we go to the office. Where you let me do the

81

talking," she told him. A quick check of the sundial outside her window showed they had about ten minutes left before fifth period ended. "And then once you're enrolled, you'll tell me who your dad is, right? I'm taking a risk here, so don't back out on me later."

"I won't," Phaeton promised. He held his middle three fingers downward, so they resembled the letter *M*. "Mortal's honor."

After scurrying through the hall, they crept down the marble staircase to the main floor, then made their way to the office. The minute they reached it, Pheme de-invisibled him.

"You're visible now, so don't do anything or go anywhere. Stay right here outside the office door until you hear me say your name," she instructed him.

"Will I get to meet Zeus?" he asked in an excited voice.

"No. Ms. Hydra is our best shot at getting what we want. Just do what I tell you, okay?"

Phaeton gave her a disappointed look but nodded.

All nine of Ms. Hydra's heads looked up when Pheme came through the door. "Hi there, Ms. Pinky," Pheme said, addressing Ms. Hydra's pink head. Although everyone knew that was her nickname, Pheme was the only student who usually called her that. She and Pinky were friends because they had something in common—a love of gossip!

Pheme held up the *Teen Scrollazine* she'd brought and waved it from side to side enticingly. "Have you read the latest about that new mortal rock star Orpheus?"

"Ooh. No! Let me see that," said Pinky. Pheme set the scrollazine on the counter, and Pinky craned her long neck to read it.

Ms. Hydra's other eight heads did the same. Most of the time they couldn't care less about the kind of tittle-tattle Pinky adored. But no one was above a little celebrity gossip from time to time. And right now Orpheus was the biggest craze ever on Earth. Lots of girls at MOA were fans too.

While Ms. Hydra's heads were distracted by the scrollazine, Pheme slipped the altered enrollment form from her pocket and placed it on top of a stack of papers on Ms. Hydra's countertop.

"Oh," Pheme said a few seconds later. "I almost forgot. I'm here to help the new boy get his textscrolls."

Ms. Hydra's grumpy green head turned to gaze at her. "What new boy?"

"Phaeton," Pheme said loudly.

On cue Phaeton entered the office. "Is this the office? I'm Phaeton, a new student. Someone told me to come here for textscrolls."

"Oh, dear! I don't recall seeing your enrollment

form," Ms. Hydra's gray head told him. It was her most efficient head, but it was also a worrywart.

Pheme pointed toward the stack on which the form sat. "Is it in there, maybe?"

"Yes, here it is," said Ms. Hydra's impatient purple head, snatching it off the top of the stack. "Odd. I don't remember seeing it before."

The green head glanced at it. "Neither do I. But one of us must've filled it out. Look at the handwriting." Luckily, the other six heads were too fascinated by the scrollazine to weigh in on the enrollment form.

Within minutes Phaeton's arms were loaded down with textscrolls for the five classes he'd be taking. After the two of them left the office and found his locker, Pheme got down to business.

"Okay. I did my part of our bargain. Now, who's your dad?" she demanded.

"Outside," Phaeton replied, nodding toward the main doors of the Academy.

Pheme looked at him in confusion. "You mean he's here? At MOA?"

Phaeton laughed. "Not exactly." He stowed his scrolls and slammed his locker door shut. "Come on," he said, grabbing her arm.

More intrigued than ever, Pheme allowed him to pull her down the hall to a window that faced west.

"Up there," said Phaeton, pointing. "See him?"

Pheme glanced upward, shading her eyes from the bright light of the sun. But there was no one in the sky as far as she could see. No one except . . .

"You mean Helios?" she guessed in surprise.

"That's right," Phaeton said proudly.

"The god of the sun? He's your dad?" she repeated, just to be sure.

"Shh!" Whipping out an arm, Phaeton waved away the cloud-letters that had puffed from her lips.

Helios was so bright that no one dared look directly upon him. Still, Pheme could make out the outline of his magnificent chariot, which carried the sun across the sky every day. If Phaeton's story was true, this was big news indeed!

"Isn't his chariot amazing?" he said excitedly. "When I finally meet him, I'm going to get him to let me drive it!"

Pheme stared at him, aghast. "But wouldn't that be dangerous? Helios's chariot is fiery hot. And it's pulled by fierce horses that breathe out flames. You know that, don't you?"

"I could handle it," Phaeton insisted, sounding cocky as usual.

Pheme just shook her head in disbelief. "But—"

Ping! Ping! Ping! The lyrebell chimed, signaling the

end of fifth period. "The school day is now over," MOA's herald announced in a self-important voice that echoed through the whole Academy. Doors flew open all along the hallway. Students began streaming out.

Pheme could feel the news about Phaeton and Helios bubbling up inside her. It would probably be smart to keep it to herself for now. At least until she could tell Zeus and get back on his good side. She wouldn't want him to get wind of the gossip and question Phaeton right away. She couldn't chance Zeus finding out that she'd helped Phaeton trick his way into enrolling at MOA.

Still, she felt like she was going to *explode* if she didn't tell someone right that second. She couldn't help it. Keeping news this big quiet was just not in her nature. After all, she was the goddessgirl of gossip. It was practically her duty to shout it to everyone in school. Just imagine their excitement! Imagine how they would listen with wide eyes, hanging on her every word!

"Um, I've got something to do," Pheme told Phaeton. "Can you find your own way to your dorm room? Fifth floor?" Turning from him, she joined the stream of students hurrying toward the Academy's front doors.

"Sure, no problem. But hey, wait," Phaeton called after her. "I still don't know your name!"

Pretending she hadn't heard him, Pheme pushed on through the doors. Outside, the pent-up gossip burst from her immediately. She flitted around the courtyard from group to group spreading her news about "the new boy." Being the one in the know and answering everyone's questions about him gave her a rush.

Even if she did get a few of her facts a little mixed up: "Yes, that's right, he's *obsessed* with chariots. And his dad is Helios. Uh-huh. The sun god! And he comes from a school on Earth called Ima Dumbhead Middle School."

Overhearing, Athena came up to her. "If he's interested in chariots, tell him I'd be happy to show him my chariot designs sometime."

"Sure," said Pheme, remembering that the chariot was one of Athena's many inventions.

"I'm kind of surprised my dad invited another mortal kid to MOA," Athena went on. "I mean, having Heracles here has worked out great, but there are some others I could name—" Her voice trailed off, and she looked over at Artemis, who was talking to a boy named Actaeon a short distance away.

Although Actaeon was mortal, Pheme figured Athena was probably thinking of a different mortal boy. One named Orion. He had only been at MOA a short time. But during his brief stay he'd caused plenty of trouble while pursuing his dream of becoming a famous actor.

In fact, he'd practically ruined one of the school plays, skipping out on his starring role when a better opportunity opened up on Earth. An opportunity that actually hadn't panned out. Served him right. Because he'd also broken Artemis's heart. A juicy bit of gossip Pheme herself had helped spread at the time.

"Did you hear that the new boy and Heracles are going to be roommates?" Aphrodite asked, coming over to them.

Athena nodded. "Heracles only just found out. I think he's gotten used to having a room to himself." She smiled. "He's so cute the way he takes care of that big knobby club of his. I wonder where he'll put it now."

"The one he uses to battle monsters?" Persephone asked, joining them too.

"Exactly," Athena said. "He told me that every night he lays it on top of his spare bed. He's so fond of that thing, I sometimes wonder if he tucks it under the blankets before he goes to sleep on the other bed."

Pheme joined in the girls' laughter at that, filing away this delectable morsel of gossip. It was so unusual for Athena to let down her guard like this. Awesome!

As if it just now dawned on her that Pheme had been there the whole time she'd been talking, Athena gave a start. "I . . . oh . . . I have to go now." She began to back away.

"Okay. Ta-ta, then," said Pheme, giving her hand a little flutter in farewell.

"Nice fingernail polish," Athena commented. "Looks kind of familiar for some reason." She scrunched up her brows, thinking.

Pheme's heart gave a hard lurch, and she yanked both

hands behind her back. Was there a hidden meaning in Athena's words? Had she guessed about Pheme reading her diaryscroll?

But Athena only smiled and said, "You should wear red more often. It looks good with your hair." Then she and her friends walked away.

"Uh, thanks," Pheme called after her. *Phew! That was too close for comfort!*

6

Caught!

P HAETON WAS AT A TABLE WITH SOME GODBOYS when Pheme got to the cafeteria for dinner that night. How nice that he was already making friends! As she passed them, Ares spoke up in a teasing voice.

"Ouch! Somebody hand me some sunglasses!" he said. "Phaeton's so bright, I've gotta wear shades!" The other godboys at the table laughed.

Catching her eye, Phaeton scowled at her. *Uh-oh!* Sounded like some of her gossip about him was making the rounds. He had to know she was responsible. This was always an awkward moment—when the gossip-ee (Phaeton) met up with the gossip-er (her).

She smiled at him weakly, pretending she didn't know what was up. Then she hurried to the cafeteria line.

The eight-handed lunch lady was ladling up bowls of celestial soup. As Pheme stood in line with a tray, her stomach growled. So far today all she'd had was breakfast and a few snacks. She was starving! After grabbing one of the eight full bowls being handed out, she started toward the table she usually shared with Medusa and Pandora.

But Phaeton was waiting for her, blocking her path. "You rat! You told!" he hissed at her. "You promised you wouldn't, but you did!"

"Shh!" Pheme darted a look beyond his shoulder. All the boys at his table and the one next to it were looking at them. Keeping her voice low so that the cloud-letters she puffed would be as small as possible, she bent close to his ear. "But I didn't actually *promise*, remember? I only said that if you shared your secret, I'd help you get into MOA. Which I did."

Unfortunately for her, his new friends had excellent eyesight. "She's the goddessgirl of gossip, dude! What did you expect?" Ares yelled from the boys' table.

"Gossip?" A vein jumped in Phaeton's throat as he studied her. He looked really upset!

A mean squinty-eyed godboy named Makhai hooted with laughter. "Telling Pheme anything is like asking the MOA herald to blast out the word to the far corners of the universe."

"Yeah, everyone knows that," Apollo added.

Everyone except Phaeton. Until now.

"You tricked me," he accused her, his face flushing an angry red. He was steaming more than her soup was!

Pheme drew back in surprise. "No, I didn't. I fulfilled my part of our deal." She did feel kind of bad about upsetting him, though. Sometimes spreading certain kinds of gossip was like eating too many Oracle-O cookies. Though tasty and enjoyable at the time, afterward you felt a little sick.

Phaeton glared at her. Then he turned to the table of godboys. "I'm not lying. Helios *is* my dad."

"Uh-huh, sure he is, *sunny* boy," said Makhai's equally mean friend, Kydoimos. "Then why doesn't your skin glitter?"

"Yeah, or why don't your eyeballs blast out rays of sunlight?" asked Makhai. The two boys cracked up laughing.

"Don't believe me?" With a defiant toss of his golden hair, Phaeton announced to the whole cafeteria, "Well, I'll *prove* it. You'll see!" Then, he stalked off toward the exit.

"Wait!" Pheme chased after him, still holding her tray. She'd only taken a couple of steps when he whirled around to face her. She stopped so suddenly that her soup sloshed over her fingers. Luckily, it wasn't hot enough to burn.

"Don't you and your big mouth dare follow me," Phaeton told her. "You ruined everything." He turned his back on her, then stomped the rest of the way across the cafeteria and out the door.

Yikes! He was really mad! Pheme set down her tray on the nearest table, then grabbed a napkin to wipe the soup from her fingers. Having witnessed all the shouting, lots of students were now staring at her. Including

Athena and her goddessgirl friends, whose table was only a few feet away.

Pheme shot Athena a nervous glance, then managed a weak smile. But Athena didn't notice. Her eyes were focused on Pheme's hand.

Pheme looked to see why. *Oh, no!* Some of the concealer had come off! A big smear of red was now exposed on her hand. It was that stupid soup. It was *water* based. *Aghhh!*

Totally panicking, Pheme crossed her arms and rammed her hands under her armpits to hide them. Athena's blue-gray eyes narrowed with suspicion. The two girls stared at each other for a long moment. Then, leaning toward her friends, Athena whispered something to them.

Pheme backed away. Turning to her tray, she pretended to fumble with her silverware. But really she was getting the concealer from her pocket. Keeping her back to Athena's table to hide what she was doing, she quickly covered up the smear of red on her hand.

When she finally turned around again, all four goddessgirls were glaring at her. The suspicion in their eyes was plain to see. Athena had guessed what she'd done, and had told her friends. Pheme was sure of it. Even Artemis's three dogs had raised their heads to eye her accusingly.

"I . . . I better go get some more soup. Mine's gone cold," she stammered, giving them a fake smile.

Suddenly Heracles got up from one of the boys' tables and came over to Athena's table. From the look on his face he must've known something was up. But he didn't ask what. Instead he just said to Athena, "I'll go check on Phaeton and make sure he's okay." Athena gave him a quick smile of thanks.

"Wait up, bud," Eros chimed in. He slung his quiver of arrows over one shoulder and casually followed Athena's crush out the cafeteria door. As he exited, he shot Pheme a look.

Before she could interpret it, Athena spoke up. "Pheme?"

"Huh?" said Pheme. Athena's eyes were glued to her again and she was waving her over. Feeling as caught as a fish with a hook in its mouth, Pheme reluctantly stepped closer to the girls' table. Her gaze flicked from Athena to Aphrodite to Artemis to Persephone. Their expressions were all condemning.

Aphrodite spoke first. "Love your nails," she said in a voice that was a little too sweet to be genuine. "Such an unusual bright red. What's the color? Its name, I mean."

Pheme balled her hands into fists, self-consciously hiding her nails. "I . . . um . . . can't remember."

"Can I borrow some of it?"

"Uh, sure," said Pheme, relaxing. "Anytime." Tonight, she'd make a quick trip to the Immortal Marketplace and get some made to match. Problem solved.

"Awesome," said Aphrodite. She rose from their table. "How about now?"

"Now?" squeaked Pheme. "Oh. Well, I don't have it with me."

"Is it in your room?" Athena asked, rising too. "We were just going up ourselves. We'll go with you to get it."

"What's the rush?" asked Pheme. "I haven't eaten yet." Not that she really felt like eating. Her stomach was churning with worry. "Besides, I think the polish was empty after I used it this morning. I probably threw it away."

"We can check your trash can and get the name off the bottle," Persephone suggested.

"Yeah, so go ahead and eat. We'll wait," said Aphrodite.

"Oh, okay," said Pheme. They were obviously on to her.

What if they ratted her out to Principal Zeus? Of course, he'd never told her she *couldn't* snoop in the girls' dorms. And he hadn't specifically banned her from reading diaryscrolls. Still, she had a strong feeling he might not approve. Especially of her spying on Athena. After all, he often called her his favorite daughter of all time.

Athena and her friends left her alone while she ate the new soup she got from the lunch lady. But she was so nervous, she only managed to eat half of it. In fact, it was a wonder she could even get the soup to her mouth, since her hand trembled each time she lifted the spoon from the bowl.

"I'm ready," she said at last.

"Much as I'd like to go with you all, I've got to meet Apollo at the archery range for practice," Artemis said. "We're leaving after lunch tomorrow for a competition down on Earth." She gave her friends a look. "I'll catch up with you later so you can fill me in, though." After she left with her dogs, the other three girls and Pheme left the cafeteria too.

As they started up the marble staircase to the fourth floor, Pheme tried to think what to do. She hardly ever wore nail polish. She knew that there were some bottles in a box on the shelf above her desk, but were any of them red? Probably not. She wouldn't be that lucky!

When they reached her room at the end of the hall, Pheme opened her door and reluctantly let Athena, Aphrodite, and Persephone inside.

"How cute!" Aphrodite exclaimed, glancing around

with interest. "Nice bedspread. And I love the framed pictures."

Pheme smiled, relaxing a little. "I have more in my clos—" She broke off, realizing what a risky thing she'd almost said. What if the girls asked to see her other pictures? They were in her spare closet. Right next to the "snoop" files she kept on everyone at MOA. Not that she saw anything wrong with snooping. But *they* might.

"Whoa," said Aphrodite. She pointed to an orange-framed picture of a blond boy with dazzling white teeth and pale blue eyes. One of many celebrity pictures on her walls. "Ye gods! What's Orion's picture doing here?"

"Well, he *is* a celebrity," Pheme said defensively. "Even if he did almost ruin the school play and break Artemis's heart."

"Let's just be glad she isn't here to see it," said Persephone.

"Why?" Instantly on the alert for a new rumor to spread, Pheme licked her orange-glossed lips. "Are you saying that even though Artemis is crushing on Actaeon now, she's still not over Orion?"

"No!" the other three girls said at the same time.

Pheme looked at them, confused. "As in no, she's still not over him?"

"No, as in no, we're not saying she's not over him," said Athena.

"We mean she *is* over Orion," said Aphrodite.

"But that doesn't mean she'd want to be reminded of him," Persephone added.

"So a reminder would be just too painful for her?" Pheme pressed.

"Just drop it, okay?" Aphrodite said with an exasperated sigh. She looked around. "Now, where's that nail polish you were going to lend me?"

"Um, I think I threw it away," Pheme hedged.

"Not in here," Persephone noted, checking the trash can under her desk.

"Oh. Well, then, I-I'm not sure where I put it," Pheme said, stalling for time.

"We'll help you look," offered Athena. She headed for the shelves by Pheme's desk. Aphrodite and Persephone started for the spare closet.

Pheme raced past the girls and threw herself against the closet. Her back was plastered against the doors, her arms dramatically outstretched.

Athena, Persephone, and Aphrodite stopped in their tracks, their eyes widening.

"Try that striped box on the shelf above my desk," Pheme told them. The words rushed out of her before she could even think to lie.

A feeling of doom washed over her as Athena lifted

the box down to Persephone, who handed it to Pheme. Reluctantly she set the box on top of her desk and opened it. As she'd expected, there were only a half dozen bottles of nail polish inside. All orange. There was every shade of orange lip gloss imaginable too.

The other three girls were looking over her shoulder. "Hmm," said Aphrodite. "Fancy that. No red polish."

"Someone must've borrowed it," Pheme said lamely. "Maybe Medusa."

"Really?" said Persephone. "I've only ever seen Medusa wear green polish."

"Still, we can go ask her," Athena said, calling Pheme's bluff. "Want to?"

Pheme shook her head. She closed the box and set it back on the shelf.

"Thought not." Aphrodite dropped into the desk

chair. Persephone sat on the bed, leaving Athena and Pheme to face off.

"You know, I just remembered something," Athena mused. "I think I saw some polish in the Immortal Marketplace that matches your nails. Hmm. What was the name of it? Oh, right!" She snapped her fingers, her eyes narrowing on Pheme. "It was called *Caught Red-Handed.*"

Pheme stumbled back from the glares the girls sent her. Feeling cornered, she lashed out at Athena. "You're just being mean because you don't like me," she blurted. "You practically said so in your dia—duh, um—" She spluttered to a stop. Pressing her lips together, she wished she could call back her words.

"I knew it! You snooped in my room," Athena accused. Her face flamed almost as red as Pheme's fingernails.

"I can't believe you! My diaryscroll is private!"

Pheme shifted into damage control mode. No way was she going to admit what she'd done. Let them prove it. She widened her eyes. "I don't know what you're talking about."

"Well, let's see what my dad has to say about this." Athena headed for the door. Aphrodite and Persephone were right behind her.

"No!" Pheme said in alarm. If Zeus got mad at her again, she could kiss any possibility of a letter of recommendation from him good-bye. In fact, he might even write a letter to *Teen Scrollazine* advising *against* choosing her for the reporter job.

He'd probably make her quit her office job with Ms. Hydra and take away her floor monitor duties too. Worse yet, what if he sent her home? Then she'd have to go back to being the ignored middle kid again!

Athena turned the doorknob, eyeing her.

"Okay, okay. It's true," Pheme admitted. "I'm sorry I snooped. But I didn't see anything interesting. Barely even read ten words," she said, fudging the truth. "Mostly just stuff about your homework assignments. So no harm done, right?"

A look of relief flitted across Athena's face. *Rats*, Pheme couldn't help thinking. Had she stopped reading too soon? Were there some juicy bits buried in that diaryscroll that she'd missed?

"If you didn't want anyone to read it, why didn't you put a magical locking ribbon around it?" Pheme asked, trying to shift the blame.

Aphrodite frowned. "She shouldn't have to!"

"Besides, I usually do hide it," said Athena. "And I did take precautions." She stared pointedly at Pheme's red-nailed fingers. "There's a spell on it, as you well know."

A little embarrassed, Pheme put her hands behind her back.

"What did you use to cover the stain?" Persephone asked curiously.

"Concealer." Pheme pulled it out of her pocket to show them. "Only, it comes off with water." Then she brightened as an idea came to her. "I'll go wash my hands, okay? And then you can reverse the spell."

"Do you really expect to get off that easily?" Aphrodite snapped.

"Yes?" Pheme lied hopefully.

"Think about it," Athena said, folding her arms. "You wouldn't like it if someone came into your room while you were gone and read *your* private stuff, would you?"

Pheme's eyes automatically darted to her spare closet's closed doors, then darted away. "Well, when you put it like that, it sounds bad, but—" She shrugged. "I'm the

112

goddess of gossip, remember? Asking me to stop snooping for gossip is like asking you to stop being brainy. Or Aphrodite to stop being beautiful. Or Persephone to stop growing flowers."

Aphrodite sniffed. "That's a cop-out. Beauty and brains don't hurt people. Gossip does."

"Not true!" argued Pheme. "Not always. Sometimes gossip is helpful. What about that time during Hero Week? Remember how I helped spread the word that you were competing with Isis—that goddessgirl from Egypt—to find a girlfriend for that annoying Pyg guy? Without me and my gossip, you might never have found potential girlfriends for him."

"Well, I guess I see your point." Aphrodite looked momentarily taken aback by her well-reasoned logic. "But more often than not your gossip causes trouble instead of helping."

Athena nodded. "Remember Freya's necklace?"

As if she could forget! "Okay, so I made a teeny little mistake," said Pheme. "You've made them too. What about those inventions you rained down on mortals when you first got to MOA? And, Persephone, didn't you misjudge your friends when you first met Hades?" She looked back at Aphrodite. "And as for you—Hello? Trojan War?"

All three girls looked surprised now. They probably hadn't realized what a good memory she had for stuff like that. *Ha! Got you there!* thought Pheme. "Now, will you help me with these hands or not?"

"I'm not sure," Athena said evenly. She exchanged looks with Aphrodite and Persephone. Then the three of them put their heads together and began to whisper.

While they were deciding her fate—at least, that's what Pheme assumed they were doing—she sweated

114

it out. With her supergood hearing, she caught a word every now and then. "Spell . . . challenge . . . Zeus . . . "

Zeus? Ye gods!

"You aren't really going to tell your dad about all this, are you?" Pheme interrupted.

They looked over at her. "You're asking *us* to keep a secret?" Persephone chided gently. "Would you? Think about it."

Pheme opened her mouth to protest that she could too keep a secret, but then she closed it again. Her shoulders slumped. "You're right. I'd probably tell," she admitted.

At this, something in Athena's stance softened. "I won't tell him," she said at last.

Pheme's eyes lit up with relief. "Thanks." She held out her hands and wiggled her fingers, hinting. "And the red?"

"I'll undo it," Athena told her.

"Awesome!" Pheme smiled, hardly believing she was being let off the hook.

"Under two conditions," added Athena.

"Not awesome," said Pheme. She flounced over to sit on her bed. "What are they?"

The other three girls sat on the spare bed across from her. Athena looked at her sternly. "First you have to promise never to snoop in anyone's room ever again."

Since Pheme had been rethinking the wisdom of this information-gathering technique anyway, she nodded easily. She'd just have to fall back on other tried-and-true methods. Like eavesdropping on conversations, listening through walls and doors, and peeking through keyholes.

"A nod isn't a promise," said Aphrodite. "Ask her to pledge an oath."

"Where's your *Goddessgirl Guide?*" asked Persephone, looking around.

Pheme got up and opened a drawer in her desk. Then she pulled out a pale pink scroll tied with a sparkly silver ribbon. The *Goddessgirl Guide* was more than just a scroll that explained MOA's rules and history. It was practically *sacred*. No one would dare break a promise made while holding it.

Grasping the scroll in both hands, she said, "I solemnly swear never again to snoop in anyone's room *when they aren't there.*"

Athena sighed at the last few words of Pheme's pledge. But she let them pass, seeming to understand that a little leeway was necessary for the goddess of gossip.

Pheme dropped the scroll onto her desk and held her hands outstretched again, hinting.

Frowning, Aphrodite folded her arms. "*Two* conditions, remember?"

"Right." Athena stood up. "So here's the hard part,

Pheme. If we agree not to tell my dad, then you have to agree to accept a challenge."

Pheme held her breath, wondering what this could mean. "What challenge?"

"I hereby challenge you to go one entire day without gossiping," Athena announced.

"Are you joking?" Pheme was so flabbergasted, she almost fell over. "What if you had to be *dumb* for a day?" she asked Athena.

"Been there," said Athena.

"Oh, yeah," said Pheme, suddenly remembering. Dumb was exactly what Athena had become for almost a week not long ago, after being bumped by a bubble from a mysterious, magical box Pandora had opened.

A silence fell in the room as Pheme considered her options. She didn't really have any. "Okay, I'll try," she agreed reluctantly.

"It won't be as hard as you think," Athena encouraged. "I have a magic spell that will help you."

"Another spell? I don't like the sound of that," said Pheme. But what choice did she have? None, that's what. Once Athena removed the red-handed spell, at least Pheme wouldn't have to walk around hiding her hands anymore. Or worry about soup sloshing on them.

"Okay. Two spells, then," Pheme agreed. "A red-removal one. And a no-gossip one." She stuck both hands out toward Athena, accepting the challenge.

And the two spells were cast.

7

Charades

WHEN PHEME WOKE THE NEXT MORNING, SHE peered into the mirror above her spare desk. She'd expected to look and feel different somehow, knowing she was now under Athena's anti-gossip spell. But she looked and felt just like her regular self. And that included normal hands, thanks to Athena's red-removal spell.

Humming a little tune, she got dressed, and then headed to the cafeteria for breakfast. On her way down the marble staircase, she passed Pandora going back up.

Before Pheme could even say hi, Pandora stopped dead and fixed her with a glare. "Athena told me what you did?" she said, making her statement sound like a question. It was something the curious girl couldn't seem to help doing, especially when she was excited or upset. Which she definitely was now!

"I can't believe you!" Pandora went on, her voice rising with anger. "You snooped in our room?"

"I'm sorry," said Pheme, meaning it. "I won't do it again. And don't worry," she added, hoping to smooth things over with her friend. "I didn't find anything. Nothing juicy, anyway."

Then, remembering the note Heracles had sent Athena with the row of *X*s and *O*s at the bottom, Pheme's brown eyes began to twinkle. "Except, there was that note Athena got from—" A sudden tickle in her throat made her cough. Then, to her embarrassment, she made some really odd sounds: *"Croak, honk!"*

She paused in surprise, then continued on. But the rest of the words she'd intended to say came out all weird: "—from a pair of fleas."

Pandora's head jerked back. "Huh? What's wrong with you?" she asked, reading the cloud-words that had formed above Pheme's head.

Pheme glanced upward too. She frowned. "Wait! That's not what I meant to say!" She'd meant to say "from Heracles" not "from a pair of fleas." She tried again, but the cough returned. And the sounds: *"Croak, honk, honk!"*

Pandora giggled uncertainly. "What's up with you today? Got a frog in your throat? Or maybe a honking goose?"

"Ha. Ha," said Pheme. "Not." Then she snapped her fingers as something dawned on her. "I get it! That spell must be mixing up my words to stop me from gossiping!"

"What spell?"

"Athena's. Didn't she tell you? She put an anti-gossip spell on me. It's just for twenty-four hours, though," Pheme explained. "I can make it."

"If you say so," Pandora said, climbing past her. "But I'm not sure I could stop being *curious* for twenty-four hours."

At least Pandora didn't sound so mad anymore, thought Pheme as she continued downstairs. She'd even sounded sort of sympathetic. Being curious about everything, she probably understood how urgently you could want to know something—or, in Pheme's case, want to *share* something.

"See you," Pheme called after her. But Pandora didn't

seem to hear her. Either that or she was still mad after all.

In the cafeteria Pheme grabbed a plate of hambrosia and eggs from the eight-armed lunch lady, then sat down at an empty table. As she began to eat, she looked around for Phaeton but didn't see him.

She hoped Heracles had managed to calm him down after he'd stormed out of the cafeteria yesterday. Maybe she should try apologizing next time she saw him. Even if she didn't exactly think she'd been wrong, since she hadn't actually broken any promises. Still, she didn't want him to hate her.

She'd almost finished eating when Medusa joined her, sliding her tray onto the table as she took the seat opposite. The dozen snakes that stuck out from the top of Medusa's head in place of hair didn't look like they'd quite woken up yet. They were snuggled together in a drowsy ball, forming a bun at the base of her neck.

"What was up with you and that new boy last night?" Medusa asked, pouring milk onto her pomegranola. "Do you really believe his wild story about Helios?"

"Well," said Pheme, "his mom did tell him that—" For the second time that morning her words strangled in her throat and she began to make weird sounds. *"Squee! Oink! Oink!"*

"—knees the bun of the fun pod," she finally finished. Of course, what she'd meant was: *His mom did tell him that he's the son of the sun god.*

Startled, Medusa almost drowned her cereal. Setting down the pitcher of milk, she peered at the cloud-words forming overhead. "'Bun of the fun pod'?" She let out a snort of laughter. "What's that supposed to mean?"

"Shh!" Pheme whispered, appalled. "Everyone's looking." She reached up and waved away the ridiculous cloud-words that had formed overhead.

When she tried again to explain what Phaeton's mother had told him, she was seized by another oinking fit.

Medusa stared at her. "Are you catching a swine flu or something?"

"No, I—" Pheme tried to continue, but more preposterous sounds and words kept puffing from her lips. "*Ribbit! Croak!* I mean she—*hissss*—told him that . . ."

Medusa's snakes began wiggling. The hissing sounds Pheme was making were disturbing them.

"Shh. It's okay, Sweetpea. Calm down, Lasso," Medusa murmured. She'd given names to all twelve of her snakes. They were like her pets or something.

"Sorry," Pheme told her. "I meant to say that . . . Athena patooee blunder a smell." (Which actually should've been: *Athena put me under a spell*.)

Pheme's cheeks flamed bright red. Students were pointing at the words drifting away over her head. Some giggled or looked confused. Others glanced at her with pity in their eyes, as if they thought she might be totally losing it.

So how come she'd been able to tell Pandora about the spell before, but now she couldn't tell Medusa? Was it possible that the spell grew stronger each time she attempted to gossip?

Medusa stood up abruptly. "I can't stay if you're going to keep hissing and spouting nonsense. You're upsetting my snakes." With that, she picked up her tray and high-tailed it to another table.

And wouldn't you know it, Athena, Aphrodite, Persephone, and Artemis were all in the cafeteria now too. They were sitting not more than a few feet away at the popular table. Witnesses to her humiliation.

Pheme grabbed her tray of half-eaten food, dropped it off at the tray return, and started out of the cafeteria. It only took a minute, but it felt like hours till she was out the cafeteria door and in the main hall.

This dumb spell was turning out to be worse than she'd expected. Maybe she should just go to her room and stay there till tomorrow. She had a variety of snacks stashed away in her closet, enough to last till morning. She could tell everyone she was sick.

Good plan, she decided. So she dashed upstairs and into her room, slamming the door behind her. Safe at last.

She opened the window by her desk and leaned her head out. Breathing the cool morning air in great gulps calmed her. And it seemed to ease her throat, which was scratchy from all that oinking and hissing.

Waaaa!

Pheme clapped a hand over her mouth, thinking she was making weird sounds again. But then she realized that the *waaaa* sound wasn't coming from her.

Waaaa! It sounded kind of like a baby crying. No, it was more like the bleat of a deer! And it was coming from overhead. She twisted to gaze skyward just in time to see a chariot, drawn by four golden-horned, milk-white deer, sail over the school.

She stared after it, confounded. Those were Artemis's deer. And that was her chariot. But Artemis was in the cafeteria. Pheme had just seen her. So who was driving her chariot?

She sucked in her breath as a possible answer came to her. Was it Phaeton? He hadn't been in the cafeteria. And he was obsessed with chariots.

But he wouldn't just take Artemis's chariot without permission. Would he? Craning her neck, Pheme tried to see the driver. It did look like a boy. Just before the chariot disappeared in the distance, she caught a glimpse of his golden hair whipping in the breeze. *Golden* hair! Like Phaeton's.

Convinced now that he was the driver, she rushed back downstairs. Artemis needed to know what was going on. Everyone knew how picky she was about that chariot and her deer. And someone needed to rein Phaeton in before an accident happened!

Besides that, Pheme wanted to share her news, because she just, well, loved being the first to share news. She imagined the hush that would fall over the room as everyone stopped what they were doing and saying to listen to what *she* had to say. And how grateful Artemis would be to her for telling what she'd seen!

When Pheme reached the cafeteria, she scanned the room for Phaeton first, just in case she'd been wrong about him and the chariot. Nope. She didn't see him. And Artemis was still at the popular table. Pheme's urge to gossip overcame any hesitation she might have felt based on what had happened every other time she'd tried it today. She dashed over.

"What's up?" Artemis asked when Pheme screeched to a halt beside her chair.

But when Pheme opened her mouth, all that came out were more of those weird sounds. *"Ruff! Ruff! Woof!"*

Oh no! Now Athena's spell was blocking her from saying really important stuff!

Artemis's dogs sniffed at her ankles as if they suspected she might be a dog in a girl disguise. Between woofs Pheme struggled to explain herself. Strange sentences puffed from her lips: "Your chair he's been bowling!" she warned Artemis.

Frustrated, Pheme tried again: "There's a cherry it in the pie bean driven by a face of tons." The craziness of the phrases was getting worse and worse!

As students read her words, the whole cafeteria rang with laughter. "Looks like my anti-gossip spell is working," Athena told her. "Sorry about all the laughing, though. I guess it's kind of embarrassing."

"Yeah, duh! Also dangerous because . . . " Pheme's eyes bugged out in alarm. She shook her head vehemently from side to side. She didn't dare speak again. Instead she snatched up Athena's blue feather pen.

After grabbing a napkin, Pheme used the pen to write what she'd wanted to say. The words "Phaeton has taken your chariot and flown away with it" were clear in her mind as she scribbled away. Without rereading what she *thought* she'd written, she hastily shoved the napkin toward Artemis.

"'Fate bacon your lariat and blown the hay with it'?" Artemis read aloud.

Tears of frustration sprang to Pheme's eyes as she realized that Athena's spell must extend to writing as well as speaking. *Double rats!*

Maybe she could act out what she wanted to say instead. She'd never taken a drama class or been very good at charades. But she had to try. Because this was no idle gossip she had to impart. It was important news!

Raising her hands to the top of her head, Pheme spread her fingers and pointed them upward to make pretend deer antlers. She bent over and ran one lap around the girls' table. Then she looked up at the ceiling, trying to indicate "sky." She glanced back at Artemis, hoping she'd gotten it.

Instead the girls all seemed totally confused. Artemis even looked like she wanted to laugh.

133

"Maybe someone should go get Principal Zeus," she heard Ares say somewhere behind her. "I think Pheme has flipped out."

There were some chuckles, but a lot of the students were starting to look more alarmed than entertained. A few of the godboys had left their table to come see what was going on. Pheme caught the look of concern on Eros's face. She hoped he didn't think she'd gone totally and completely insane.

Just then Athena stood up. Stepping to Pheme's side, she gave her a quick hug. "Listen up, everyone," she announced to the whole cafeteria. "Pheme's okay. It's just that she's accepted a challenge to go twenty-four hours without gossiping."

It was nice of Athena to offer a hug and explain about the challenge. And also to leave out what had led up to it, thought Pheme. But Athena—and probably everyone else here as well—didn't seem to have a clue that sometimes gossip might actually be useful to hear!

"And she even let me put her under a spell that renders any attempt at gossip impossible. Brave of her, huh?" Athena said with a smile that encouraged others to agree. "So, while she may be saying or doing some odd things throughout the day today, please just ignore them."

"Honestly," Pheme said, huffing a big sigh. "I'm just trying to explain that—*Meow! Meow!*" As more animal sounds rolled off her tongue, Artemis's dogs couldn't take it anymore. They leaped on Pheme, bracing their front paws against her, and began to bark.

"Stop, guys! She's a girl, not a cat. I promise," Artemis yelled at them.

Desperate, Pheme hopped onto the table, scattering dishes as she tried to get away from the dogs. Just then the lyrebell chimed a warning that first period was about to begin. Students were reluctant to leave the show. But when Artemis called off her dogs, everyone began to go to class.

As Artemis headed off with her dogs, Pheme climbed down from the table. She felt incredibly frustrated. She must've looked it too, because Aphrodite gave her a sympathetic smile. "This is really hard for you, isn't it?" she said. "But it *is* a fitting punishment."

"Kind of like the ones Hades gives out in the Underworld," Persephone added in a kind voice.

"Only about fourteen hours to go till bedtime. Next thing you know it'll be morning. And then the spell's over!" Athena smiled at Pheme, obviously hoping her pep talk was helping.

"Thanks," Pheme told her, even though it wasn't. But she knew Athena meant well.

Aphrodite and Athena were in Hero-ology class with her first period. However, after what had just happened, Pheme didn't feel like walking with them. And she needed to think. So she lagged behind the other two girls as they all started down the hall.

She should've dragged Artemis outside to show her that her chariot was gone from its usual spot, she realized. Too late now. Besides, the spell probably would have found a way to stop her from doing that. It did seem to be getting more powerful—and bossy—as time passed.

Anyway, maybe Phaeton had only "borrowed" the chariot for a short ride and had already returned it. Or maybe it hadn't been him driving the chariot at all. She'd made mistakes before. Like with Freya's necklace.

But she'd seen *someone* with golden hair flying away in Artemis's chariot. Unless not being able to gossip was giving her hallucinations!

8

Alike

NO WAY SHE'LL MAKE IT TWENTY-FOUR HOURS!"

Pheme overheard someone murmur this as she took

her seat in Hero-ology class. He probably thought she

couldn't hear what he was saying. Not many students

knew just how exceptional her hearing was. It was one

of the few secrets she kept pretty well, since it made her

more effective as the goddess of gossip and rumor.

Eavesdropping now, Pheme learned that most of the students around her believed she wouldn't survive Athena's no-gossiping challenge without going totally bonkers. Some thought she'd *already* gone bonkers.

It felt strange to be the object of rumors, instead of the source of them. She just hoped her teacher, Mr. Cyclops, wouldn't call on her to answer any questions today. She couldn't trust herself not to say something that Athena's spell would consider to be gossip. And how embarrassing would that be if she started making animal sounds again!

Pheme listened as the teacher droned on about Greek city-states and Spartans and blah, blah, blah. He was oblivious to the undercurrent of whispers zipping around the room.

She doodled in her notescroll while pretending to listen intently to his lecture. Acting as if she were totally unaware of—or didn't give a hoot about—what others were saying about her. But deep down inside, she really did care.

If only magic were allowed in class so she could make herself invisible. She'd always hated being ignored worse than anything. But she didn't like this kind of attention. Not one bit. Still, what could she do about it? That was the worst part. Not being able to defend herself.

Sensing someone's eyes on her, she glanced up. Eros had turned in his seat, two rows ahead of her. He was gazing at her with a thoughtful look on his face. He smiled when he caught her eye, and then motioned to her notescroll. She smiled back uncertainly. Was he asking to see her doodles?

Hiding behind the girl in front of her, Pheme held up her notescroll, tilting it so he could see what she'd drawn, but Mr. Cyclops wouldn't. Mostly they were just squiggles, but also a heart with wings, and an arrow stuck in a target. They were just doodles illustrating snippets of ideas. Plus some jotted notes for news stories. They didn't mean anything.

Still, Eros grinned when he saw them and gave her a thumbs-up. It was as if he saw something in them that she didn't. She remembered the look of relief that had flitted across his face when Athena had explained to everyone in the cafeteria about the twenty-four-hour challenge. It was nice of him not to *want* to believe she was crazy.

"Eros!" Mr. Cyclops called out just then. "Please pay attention. To something other than Pheme."

Eros's cheeks flamed redder than usual, and his glorious golden wings fluttered a little as he whipped around to face forward again. Pheme could feel her cheeks going red too. Sometimes Mr. Cyclops showed no sensitivity to students' feelings whatsoever!

A few titters ran through the class. Mr. Cyclops scowled. The single, humongous eye in the middle of his forehead swept the room, pinning everyone to their seats. All laughter ceased immediately, and he continued with his lecture.

At the end of class Pheme sped out ahead of Athena and Aphrodite. They'd been shooting her concerned looks from across the room. She didn't want to listen to them trying to make her feel better about the rumors of her going bonkers, if that was their plan.

Eros waited for Pheme in the hallway. "Frog still stuck in your throat?" he teased gently.

"Ribbit!" Pheme replied, shooting him a half smile.

He laughed and fell into step beside her as they moved down the hall. She let him, because for some reason he didn't annoy her like everyone else did right now.

"It's not fair of Athena to ask you to go for a day

without gossiping," he told her. "At least in my humble opinion. I mean, you're the goddess of gossip and rumor. It's what you do!" He shifted the textscrolls he was carrying from one arm to the other. "I don't get why you accepted her challenge. You could still back out, you know."

Oh, no I can't, she thought. She didn't tell him that, though. He'd probably think less of her if he knew the reason for the challenge. That she'd been caught snooping in Athena and Pandora's room!

"I—um—need to stop at my locker," she mumbled.

"Sure, no problem," he replied, following her there. What was up? He never did that. She spun the dial, opened her locker, and shoved her Hero-ology textscroll inside. Meanwhile Eros waited beside her as if it was something he did every day.

Pheme felt him staring and looked over. "What?" she asked. "Is something wrong with my hair?"

"No. Looks awesome, as usual," he said, surprising her. "Orange is my favorite color."

She felt herself blushing. "Uh . . . thanks. Mine too." No boy had ever said anything like that to her before! She dug around in her locker while he continued to stand there. Finally she asked bluntly, "Why are you hanging around me?"

He slouched against the locker next to hers. "Because I think we're a lot alike," he said.

"Because we both like orange?"

Eros laughed. "No. Because we both try to help people. I help them fall in love. You help make them famous. Or infamous," he teased with good humor. "The thing is we both use our special talents to do things on behalf of others."

Finding what she needed, Pheme pulled the text-scrolls for her next two classes from her locker. "True."

She'd never heard anyone call what she did a "special talent" before. It was nice to hear.

"And we have something else in common," Eros told her. "If anything goes wrong when we use our talents, guess who gets the blame?"

"Us!" Pheme exclaimed, slamming her locker shut. They shared a smile. For once someone seemed to understand the situation she so often found herself in.

"Hey." He bent and picked up a sheet of papyrus from the floor. "You dropped this," he said, glancing at it as he handed it to her. "A job application?"

She shrugged, reopened her locker, rammed the sheet inside, and then slammed the locker shut again. "I'm hoping to get the student staff reporter job with *Teen Scrollazine*," she admitted a little shyly as they set off down the hall, walking side by side.

"Cool. They'd be lucky to get you."

"Thanks," she said, delighted by his response. "It's not a for-sure thing. I still need to get a letter of recommendation from Principal Zeus. I'll wait till tomorrow to ask, though, after this spell ends. Then, fingers crossed."

By tomorrow she'd be able to report to Zeus about Phaeton, his chariot-borrowing, and his claims about Helios. Without oinking or croaking! Surely that would put her back on his good side so he'd write that letter. She only hoped he didn't find out about her enrolling Phaeton before she could explain it in a way that didn't make her look bad—something she hadn't exactly figured out how to do yet.

Ping! Ping! Ping! As the warning lyrebell for second period began to chime, Eros came back to their earlier topic. "So what's up with that no-gossip challenge, anyway? Why'd you accept it? Does Athena have some hold over you?"

Pheme hesitated. Something made her want to confide in him. But embarrassment and a fear that her words wouldn't come out right while she was under Athena's spell stopped her. "I—I can't tell you," she said at last.

"Aha!" he said. "Then I bet that means I'm right." His forehead wrinkled in thought. "You know, there could be a way around the challenge."

They came to a stop, since they needed to start down different hallways. She cocked her head at him, intrigued. "What do you mean?"

Eros reached out to tap her notescroll. "In the cafeteria you tried writing what you wanted to say, right?"

"Didn't work, though," she said.

He started heading off down his hall, walking backward so he still faced her. "Next time maybe try doodling what you want to say—like you were doing in

Hero-ology." Giving her a quick wave, he turned and took off for his next class.

As she hurried the rest of the way to Beauty-ology class, Pheme thought about what he'd suggested. It was worth a try.

She'd brought the concealer she'd borrowed with her, so she replaced it before heading for her seat. Medusa glanced at her a little warily as she sat down beside her at their worktable at the back of the room.

"Don't worry. I'm not going to start hissing or anything," Pheme told her.

Medusa relaxed, grinning. "I guess you can't help it. How many more hours till the spell ends?"

"Twenty-one maybe? It started at dawn this morning before I woke up and ends tomorrow at dawn. So I'll live," Pheme told her. "I think."

As the lyrebell rang to start second period, their

148

teacher, Ms. ThreeGraces, stepped to the front of the room. Her styled hair and makeup were perfect, of course. She'd probably never even once gotten a single wrinkle in her chiton before, thought Pheme.

Extending her hand, Ms. ThreeGraces gestured as gracefully as a ballerina toward a table at the front of the room. It was covered with colorful assorted flowers.

Speaking in elegant tones, she said, "We are fortunate that Persephone's mother has donated all of these blossoms for our use in class today." Persephone's mom owned a flower shop called Demeter's Daisies, Daffodils, and Floral Delights in the Immortal Marketplace.

Flower arranging? Pheme scribbled the question on her textscroll. She nudged Medusa, pointing at what she'd written.

"I hope so. My snakes love the greens," Medusa

whispered back. "But I don't know. Those blossoms look like they have awfully short stems."

Pheme craned to look. She could name some of the flowers on the table—roses, daisies, poppies, hyacinths, orchids, and baby's breath. But Persephone, who was the goddess of spring, could likely have named them all.

"Today you'll be weaving blossoms with other items I'll provide to make decorative hair ornaments," Ms. ThreeGraces explained.

Hair ornaments? Pheme made a *yikes* face. Most of the girls at MOA had long hair. But she wore hers in a short, spiky style she didn't have to fuss with. She couldn't have long hair hanging over her ears. It might make her miss some news, despite her exceptional hearing!

Ms. ThreeGraces passed out bins containing pieces of lace and netting, ribbons, feathers, beads, and other knickknacks. One bin for each table: Then she excused the girls table by table to go to the front of the room for flowers.

When it was her table's turn, Pheme just grabbed a random handful and hurried back. Medusa was pickier, choosing blossoms that still had leaves. For her snakes to snack on, Pheme supposed.

Back at their table Pheme toyed aimlessly with the blossoms she'd selected. She didn't want to wear flowers in her hair. That just wasn't her style.

So while everyone else was working and her teacher's attention was on other tables, she opened her notescroll. Using her favorite orange feather pen, she scribbled a quick sketch of Artemis's chariot, then slid it over to Medusa to see if she'd be able to tell what it was.

"It's a chariot. So?" Medusa said. The green girl was making twelve ribbon and flower designs—to decorate each of the snakes that grew from her head, Pheme assumed.

Medusa tossed some leaves she'd stripped from the blossoms into the air to feed her snakes. They snapped up every bite. But when they ventured near the flowers, Medusa nudged them away. "Flowers are for dessert. After class."

Pheme slid back her chariot doodle and studied it. So far so good. She'd been half afraid the spell would alter her drawing somehow. Or, since she wasn't a real artist, that Medusa just wouldn't be able to tell what she'd drawn. But it was looking like Eros's idea might turn out to be a great one. She quickly added four deer to the chariot to identify it as belonging to Artemis.

"Why do those dogs have tree branches growing out of their heads?" Medusa asked when Pheme showed her the changes she'd made.

Before Pheme could reply, Ms. ThreeGraces appeared at her side. She'd glided over so quietly that there was no way Pheme could've heard her coming, despite her supergood hearing.

"May I see that, please?" the teacher asked, holding out her hand for the notescroll. Though Ms. Three-Graces had phrased her question as a polite request, Pheme knew there was only one acceptable response. She handed over the notescroll.

Ms. ThreeGraces took it, barely glancing at the drawing. "I'll just keep this on my desk till the end of class, shall I? So you can turn your attention to your class work." She looked pointedly at the pile of untouched blossoms on the table in front of Pheme.

Rats, thought Pheme. But then she had an idea. "I was going to add that drawing to my ornament," she fibbed. Aware that girls at nearby tables were beginning to dart looks her way, she squirmed in her chair, hoping Ms. ThreeGraces would be satisfied and leave. She'd had enough unwanted attention today, thank you very much!

"Oh!" Ms. ThreeGraces looked startled. "Well, then." She set the notescroll back on Pheme's desktop. "Carry on."

Pheme genuinely liked Ms. ThreeGraces and hated to disappoint her, so she dutifully got to work. She cut out her chariot and deer drawing, snatched up a bedraggled orange poppy, a couple of bent yellow feathers, and a scraggly piece of baby's breath. After fixing them onto a hair clip, she rammed the ornament into her hair.

There. Done! She was now wearing a ridiculous hair doohickey that wasn't her style. Which just made her day that much more perfect.

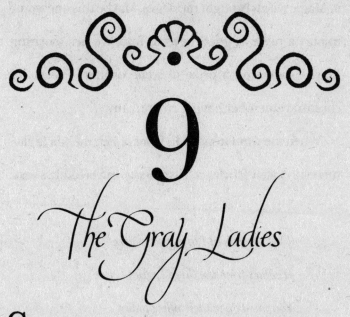

9

The Gray Ladies

SECONDS LATER THE DOOR TO THE BEAUTY-
ology room blew open. A magic wind rushed in.

Summons for Pheme! it roared. Stray blossoms, ribbons, and bits of sparkly stuff swirled up in the air in a
mini craft-material-tornado as the wind headed toward
Pheme's table at the back of the room.

Ignoring the eyes that turned her way, Pheme awaited

it. Magic winds brought messages. Maybe this one would impart a piece of good news to improve her morning. Maybe she'd won a prize in some contest! Except she couldn't remember having entered any.

When the wind stopped in front of her, the whole class turned to watch. It delivered its message in a breathless voice:

> *This command I bring your way–*
>
> *It comes from the three Ladies Gray.*
>
> *You must go to their office today.*
>
> *You must depart without delay!*
>
> *Medusa will take you.*
>
> *She knows the way.*

Having said what it came to say, the wind whooshed out the door as quickly as it had entered. Pheme and Medusa looked at each other.

"What did you do?" Medusa asked in a whisper. Pheme could remember when Medusa had been called to the Gray Ladies' office not long ago, and she'd asked Medusa the same question. Now the situation was reversed.

The Gray Ladies were the school counselors, and as everyone knew, they only summoned you to their office if you were in trouble. Had word about her breakfast time looneyness prompted this summons? Or had the counselors somehow found out about her snooping in Athena's diaryscroll? Athena had promised not to tell Zeus about it, but she hadn't promised not to tell anyone else!

"Godsamighty. Could this day get any worse?" Pheme mumbled, ignoring Medusa's question. Whatever the reason for the summons, she couldn't ignore it. And she had to go *now*. School rule.

Ms. ThreeGraces had been helping some girls at

another table with their hair ornaments when the wind had blown in. Now she called out to Pheme and Medusa. "Go on, girls. You're excused. Take some cloaks from the costume area. It'll be chilly on the trip."

"C'mon," said Medusa, jumping up from their table. Her snakes were now each wearing ribbons and flowers, which looked kind of adorable, actually. And Pheme was wearing her not-so-adorable chariot hair thingie.

Before they dashed out the classroom door, they each chose a warm cloak. Pheme's was orange wool with black toggle closures. Medusa chose—surprise—a *green* one with a hood.

Pheme had planned to find Artemis between classes so she could show her the drawing—um, hair ornament— she'd made. She'd hoped it would finally get her message across. Now it looked like she'd have to wait until she was back from the counselors' office.

"Let's stop at our lockers and stash our textscrolls so we won't have to carry them," Medusa suggested as the girls made their way down the hall.

"Good idea," said Pheme.

After their lockers they headed for the Academy's entrance. There the girls shucked off their regular sandals and grabbed winged ones from the big basket by the bronze doors.

The counselors' office was a long way away, in the far north. Luckily, the winged sandals would allow them to travel ten times faster than normal walking speed. The whole trip shouldn't take more than two hours or so.

As soon as the girls were outside, they slipped the sandals on. Laces immediately twined around Pheme's ankles. The silver wings at her heels began to gently flap.

She rose to hover in the air, just a few inches above the ground. The wings on Medusa's sandals stayed stubbornly still, however. Because she was mortal, she couldn't make them fly on her own. She'd have to hold hands with an immortal to make them work.

Knowing how sensitive Medusa could be about needing help, Pheme simply grabbed her hand. The minute their palms touched, the wings on Medusa's sandals began to flap, and she rose too.

"I don't know why, but flying in these things always makes me nervous," Pheme said. It wasn't true, but she hoped it would make Medusa feel better. "Don't let go, okay?"

"Don't worry. I won't!" Medusa said sincerely. "These things make me nervous too."

As the girls skimmed across the courtyard, Pheme suddenly noticed Artemis's chariot. There it was—in its usual spot at the side of the school. The sun glinted off the golden horns of Artemis's white deer as they grazed.

What a relief! Looked like she'd been worried for nothing. If Phaeton really had taken the chariot, he was back now.

Good thing. Nobody flew Artemis's chariot but her. She would be furious if an unskilled driver dared to!

Soon the two girls were flying high, hand in hand, their cloaks whipping in the wind. Medusa pulled up her hood to keep her snakes warm.

"How far north is the counselors' office?" Pheme asked. "I've never been there before."

"We keep going till we get goose bumps," said Medusa.

"Pretty strange directions," said Pheme.

"Yeah, well, you haven't seen anything yet," said Medusa.

What did that mean? wondered Pheme. "So, what are the Gray Ladies like? What happened when you went to see them?"

Medusa shrugged. "They helped. I didn't think they could, but they did. Just try to ignore how weird they are."

Weird? They flew on in silence as Pheme considered this. The Gray Ladies were a big mystery to anyone who hadn't been to their office. No one who ever had been to see them discussed what happened there. After Medusa had gone, Pheme had tried to get her to explain why she'd been summoned, but Medusa had kept mum.

Suddenly Pheme was almost looking forward to this visit. The experience might make for a good news article in *Teen Scrollazine*!

The air around them gradually became chilly. Soon Pheme began to shiver in spite of her wool cloak. Noticing, Medusa said, "We're getting close."

Pheme glanced down. A gray-black sea dotted with icebergs churned about thirty feet below them. Moments later Medusa pointed to an igloo perched atop a gigantic iceberg. Carved in the roof of the igloo were the words: "Office of the Gray Ladies."

Together the girls dipped low, slowing when their feet touched down.

"Ye gods!" Pheme exclaimed as her legs almost slid out from under her. "It's slippery!" After loosening her sandals' laces, Pheme looped the laces around the silver wings to stop their flapping so she could walk at normal speed.

"This way," Medusa told her. Still holding hands, they slipped and slid across the ice, all the way to the igloo's entrance. Pheme was surprised at how warm it was once they were inside.

A long tunnel took them to a little waiting room. Medusa pointed to a door beyond it marked ENTER. "The Gray Ladies' office is in there," she said as she hung her cloak on a coat hook on the wall. "I'll wait for you here."

She flopped down in a chair, then picked up a scrolla-zine from a side table.

Just then a voice sounded from beyond the door causing Pheme to jump. "Goddess of gossip, you may enter!" the voice commanded.

Pheme went to the door and then hesitated, glancing over at Medusa. "So I should just—"

"Go on in," Medusa finished for her. "It's okay. It's just a regular office. And they don't bite." She grinned. "Be hard to, since they only have one tooth among them."

Was she serious? Feeling a little more nervous about this whole counseling thing than she'd care to admit, Pheme pushed the door open. Once she was through it, it automatically shut behind her.

"Whoa!" She grabbed on to a rail along the wall to keep from falling. To her surprise the office floor was a big oval sheet of thick ice! And there were three lady-size haystack-looking lumps of scraggly gray moss skating around it, doing stunts.

An ice-skating rink? Medusa was crazy if she thought this was a normal office! Music blared from speakers, and a rotating mirrored ball hung from the ceiling at the center of the rink. The multifaceted ball reflected the light and sent sparkling rays of it spinning crazily around the room.

Pheme stood like a deer caught in torchlights as the three haystack lumps zoomed toward her across the rink's icy surface. There was a small haystack, a tall one, and a medium-size one that was about Pheme's height.

The tall-lump lady broke away from the other two and extended a hay-covered hand to Pheme. A single large tooth flashed white in her face as she smiled. "Grab on!" she yelled.

165

Pheme did as instructed, and was immediately pulled farther onto the ice. She glanced down at her sandals and saw they'd been magically transformed into skates. But she didn't know how to skate! Still the lady somehow kept her going as they whipped around the rink, hay-covered hand in goddessgirl hand.

"Pass me the eye, Sister!" Pheme's tall-lump partner called out suddenly.

The medium-size lump caught up to them. As if they were in a relay race, she handed off a round white eyeball instead of a baton to the tall lump. *Eew!* The eyeball made a squishy sound as the tall-lump lady popped it into her face. *Double eew!*

So these were the Gray Ladies, Pheme thought as she struggled to keep pace with her partner. Their gray tangled haystack hair was so long, it brushed the ice as they whirled and twirled. Did they have legs under there? Who knew? And how did the other two manage to skate without falling as long as Pheme's partner possessed the only eyeball in sight?

Pheme couldn't wait to get back to MOA so she could tell everyone about these oddball-eyeball counselors. *But wait,* she thought. Because of Athena's anti-gossip spell, she wouldn't be able to until tomorrow. Besides, did she really want to remind everyone that she'd been to the counselors' office?

While she'd been thinking, the eyeball's big gray iris had been peering at her intently. "When in doubt, don't shout it out," the tall Gray Lady advised.

Surprised, Pheme slipped on the ice and nearly fell. Had the counselor read her mind? she wondered as she regained her balance.

Now the tall Gray Lady plucked the tooth from her face and passed it to the medium-size Gray Lady, who stuck it on her own face. So Medusa hadn't been kidding about the shared tooth—it was just as portable as the eye!

As soon as the tooth was in place, the medium Gray Lady was able to speak. "The eye, too, Sister. So I can see her!" Instantly the tall one popped out the eyeball and tossed it back to her sister. Pheme slid on past the medium-size Gray Lady as she popped it in.

Catching up to Pheme easily, the medium Gray Lady skated backward to face her. "Where are your wings, dearie?" she asked as they skated on.

"Wings?" Pheme repeated. "I don't have any."

The eyeball blinked. Medium-lump lady stared at Pheme for a few moments, looking confused. Then she said, "Base your decisions on the greater good." Having uttered this piece of advice, she quickly handed off the tooth and the eye to the small Gray Lady, who whizzed by just then.

Squish! Small-lump lady popped in the eyeball. *Click!* She shoved in the tooth. Then she circled around to Pheme and skated smoothly beside her as the other two counselors dropped back to perform twirls, jumps, and figure eights.

The small Gray Lady sucked on the tooth as she gazed at Pheme. At last she said, "Accept your imperfections."

"You mean like not having wings?" Pheme asked.

But it seemed the small lady had no intention of explaining. All she said was, "You'll understand when the time is right. Just remember what we've told you and all will be well."

Taking Pheme's arm, she picked up speed, whizzing her around and around the rink. Then she released Pheme, sending her zooming full speed toward the exit door. "You may go now!" the small lady called after her.

Pheme cringed. She was hurtling toward the door

with no way to stop herself. She was going to crash into it!

But when she was only a few feet away, the door magically swung open on its own. Startled, she slid all the way out to the waiting room, her arms spinning wildly. Medusa squeaked in surprise as Pheme landed in her lap, knocking the scrollazine she'd been reading out of her hands.

"Sorry about that," Pheme said breathlessly. "Slipped on the ice. Couldn't stop."

"Ice?" said Medusa, looking puzzled. "What ice?"

"You know," said Pheme, hopping up. "The skating rink in the Gray Ladies' office?" She pointed toward her skates, but they'd already transformed back to sandals again.

"Oh, I get it," said Medusa. "It's Athena's spell, right? You're speaking nonsense again."

As they left the igloo and headed back outside, Pheme tried to convince Medusa about the skating rink.

But Medusa claimed it really had been a normal office when she'd visited.

"Maybe everyone who visits sees it differently," Pheme suggested.

"Could be," Medusa conceded. "Maybe the Gray Ladies magically change it for every student who comes here. To distract us so we'll keep our guards down and listen to their advice."

"Yeah, maybe," said Pheme. "Well, it was weird, that's for sure. I mean, I would've thought school counselors would discuss things with you before they offered advice. Those ladies were not at all what I expected. They're—" Pheme started to say. But then a tickle came into her throat, and a few duck *quacks* slipped out.

"Strange? Messy? Eyeball-limited? Dentally challenged?" Medusa supplied smoothly when Pheme couldn't continue.

Pheme laughed. "All of the above." Although, she did kind of think they were quacks, too, come to think of it. Their advice had not been at all helpful, in her opinion.

"Let me guess," Medusa went on. "They didn't ask you anything about school or your problems, right?"

"Exactly."

"Same here. I've decided they somehow already know all that stuff before they summon us to their office."

Pheme nodded. "Maybe you're right."

"And you might be surprised," Medusa added mysteriously. "Their advice could turn out to be more helpful than you expect." It was as if she'd guessed what Pheme had been thinking before!

As they flew back over the dark ocean, a silence fell between the two girls.

Pheme was starting to understand why most students didn't talk about their visits to the counselors. If she tried to explain how crazy that place was to someone who'd never been there, they probably wouldn't believe her! And she really didn't want to talk about the weird advice she'd gotten—to Medusa or anyone else.

Eventually the girls started chatting about other things, including boys. Medusa talked about Dionysus—he was her crush. In fact, she did most of the talking, since Pheme couldn't gossip.

"Dionysus says that Eros likes you," Medusa announced when they were nearing MOA again.

"What?" Pheme exclaimed. Though she'd already been starting to wonder if Eros might like her, it was kind of shocking to have Medusa come right out and say it. "Why do you think he said that?"

Medusa snorted. "Eros chose you to accompany him down the aisle at Zeus and Hera's wedding, didn't he?"

"Only by chance," Pheme said. "His arrow hit my

173

name, but it could just as easily have hit another."

"Ha!" said Medusa. "Dionysus told me that Eros *aimed* for the slip of papyrus with your name on it."

"Oh!" Now that Pheme thought about it, that kind of made sense. Eros was a crack shot as an archer. He could have hit any name he'd wanted to. Even from fifty paces. *Was* he really crushing on her? She wasn't sure she had time for a crush. She was too busy.

As they neared the Academy, Pheme noticed that Artemis's chariot and deer were gone again. That wasn't alarming, though. Artemis had said she had an archery competition down on Earth after lunch today. So she must've taken her chariot herself.

"It's almost fifth period," said Medusa. Pheme glanced at the sundial in the courtyard and saw she was right. They'd missed two class periods plus lunch. The girls said quick good-byes as they changed out of their winged sandals. Since Medusa's next class was by the Beauty-ology classroom, she took both cloaks to drop them off.

Pheme stopped by her locker before racing to Revenge-ology. Since she'd ditched yesterday to help Phaeton enroll, she dared not be late today. Ms. Nemesis was mega-strict about skipping and tardiness—and pretty much everything else.

Pheme had a ready supply of re-admittance slips she'd snitched from Ms. Hydra's wastebasket, though. If Ms. Nemesis gave Pheme any grief, she'd just zip upstairs and grab one.

Aphrodite and Eros were chatting just outside the classroom door up ahead. "I'm surprised you're here," Aphrodite was saying to him. "I thought you'd be at the archery competition with Artemis and Apollo."

"Only the top two archers were invited. They both

beat me out," Eros told her good-naturedly. Just then someone in the classroom called to Aphrodite. As she went inside the room, Eros noticed Pheme.

Smiling at her, he then nodded toward her hair. "Interesting hair thingie."

"Huh?" said Pheme. She reached up and felt her hair. "Oh, yeah. Thanks. We made them in Beauty-ology." She'd forgotten about that silly chariot-doodle flower ornament. She was surprised that it hadn't blown away during her and Medusa's trip. If only. She slipped it from her hair and tucked it into the pocket of her chiton.

Eros was looking at her curiously now. "Didn't see you at lunch."

Pheme thought about lying about where she'd been, but plenty of people knew already. Feeling a bit embarrassed, she said, "I went to see the Gray Ladies."

Eros's brows rose. "Cool."

"Freezing, actually," Pheme corrected him. "They're way far north."

"Ha!" Eros laughed. "Good one."

Oh, thought Pheme, he'd meant the *other* kind of "cool." Well, she liked that he thought she'd meant to be funny. And she also liked that he didn't think a visit to the counselors was any big deal. Had he been there himself? she wondered.

Before she could ask, he said, "Didn't see your friend Phaeton at lunch either, so I thought—" He broke off and rammed his hands into the pockets of his tunic.

Her *friend* Phaeton? She barely knew that boy!

"Heracles is sort of worried about him," Eros added quickly.

"Why?" asked Pheme, going on alert.

Eros frowned, rushing an explanation as the lyrebell began to sound. "Because Phaeton kept saying at lunch

177

how he was going to prove Helios was his dad. Said he had figured out a way to get to his palace and was planning to go. And when I saw Heracles in the hall a minute ago, he said Phaeton hadn't shown for fourth-period Revenge-ology."

A feeling of foreboding settled over Pheme as she and Eros headed into the classroom. "Do you by any chance know if Apollo and Artemis drove her chariot to their archery competition?" she asked, trying to sound casual.

"The competition isn't far, only halfway down Mount Olympus. So they went by winged sandal," he said as they took seats across from each other.

Pheme instantly imagined the worst. Foolhardy Phaeton must have flown off in Artemis's chariot to search for Helios. Was he crazy? He could get himself fried to a crisp!

Suddenly Pheme remembered something Phaeton

had told her about Helios and his chariot. Phaeton had said: "When I finally meet him, I'm going to get him to let me drive it!"

"Ye gods!" she exclaimed.

"What's the matter?" Eros asked as she jumped from her desk.

"I just remembered something I need to do," she mumbled hastily. Understatement! She had to stop Phaeton, because he was headed for disaster. "Tell Ms. Nemesis I have to miss class again today," she added. Then she scooted out the door, leaving Eros gaping after her in surprise.

Her thoughts kept pace with her feet as she scurried down the hall. Surely Helios wouldn't allow an inexperienced driver like Phaeton to carry the sun across the sky in his golden chariot.

That would be *waaay* too dangerous. If the chariot

went out of control, it could crash. Then the Earth would catch fire. And the sun's light, upon which all life on Earth was dependent, would burn itself out!

But if Helios refused Phaeton's request, that boy might just "borrow" the sun god's chariot without permission. He'd taken Artemis's, after all—twice!

She needed to tell Zeus her suspicions and fears. This was just the sort of thing he'd *want* her to report. But as she neared his office, her feet slowed. If he found out she'd sneaked Phaeton into MOA, she'd be in real trouble.

As Pheme wrestled with her thoughts, the advice of the medium Gray Lady popped into her head: "Base your decisions on the greater good."

Regardless of the consequences to herself, she *had* to tell Zeus, she realized. For the greater good of the entire Earth. Because if Phaeton got hold of Helios's chariot, there was no way he'd be able to control those fiery horses!

Fueled by fear Pheme ran down the hall. She burst into the outer office, and blurted: *"Hee-haw! Hee-haw!"*

All nine of Ms. Hydra's heads turned to look at her in surprise.

Oh, no! That stupid spell again! The welfare of the entire planet, not to mention MOA, was at stake. But she couldn't form the words to warn anyone. What was she going to do?

10

A Journey

PHEME RAN PAST MS. HYDRA TO PRINCIPAL ZEUS'S office door and knocked.

"Principal Zeus is out just now. I'm not really sure when he'll be back. Is there anything I can do to help you?" Ms. Hydra's blue head asked. This head was her sympathetic one.

"Remember that new boy I was here with yesterday?" Pheme asked.

The blue head looked at her blankly.

"I do," Ms. Hydra's grumpy green head put in. "The one none of us recalled enrolling."

"Yes, well . . . " Pheme didn't really want to open up that can of worms.

Desperate, she decided her only option was to leave Zeus a message. So as poor as they were, she'd just have to rely on her doodling skills to relay her suspicions. She pulled her hair ornament from her pocket, plucked her chariot doodle from it, and then set it on the counter.

"Can I borrow a pen and a sheet of papyrus?" she asked. After Ms. Hydra handed both to her, Pheme clipped the chariot doodle hair-thingie in the middle of the papyrus.

Using the borrowed pen, she added a stick figure of a boy on the papyrus sheet. She put him right next to her chariot doodle, so he looked like he was driving the chariot. Then, a few inches over his head, she drew the sun with lots of rays coming out from it.

Several of Ms. Hydra's heads watched curiously as she drew. "This is that new boy, Phaeton," Pheme explained.

She was relieved when her words came out exactly the way she meant them. She'd been afraid Athena's spell would interpret them as gossip. You just never knew with that spell. When it came to what was gossip and what wasn't, she often didn't agree with it. But the spell was the boss right now, so she had to be careful.

Ms. Hydra's worrywart gray head frowned at the stick figure of Phaeton. "He's very thin," it said anxiously. "He should eat more."

"Poor dogs," said the blue head. "Why did that boy tie them to the table?"

Pheme gritted her teeth but tried to remain calm. "Those are deer," she said, pointing. "That's a chariot."

"Oh!" the heads that were watching chorused in surprise.

"Could you give this drawing to Zeus the exact second he gets back?" she asked urgently. "Tell him it's an emergency. Tell him Phaeton . . . " Unfortunately, her next words stuck in her throat and she began to sputter nonsense.

As cloud-words drifted upward, all nine of Ms. Hydra's heads swiveled on their long necks to read them.

"'Jazz onto squeal the fun carry it'?" her grumpy green head read aloud. "Is that supposed to be funny?"

Of course, what Pheme had tried to say was, *Tell him Phaeton has gone to steal the sun chariot.*

Pheme turned and ran for the door. "Just give Principal Zeus my drawing? Please?" She'd have to hope he'd do a better job of interpreting it than Ms. Hydra's heads had done.

In the meantime she was going after Phaeton herself. If the entire Earth was destroyed, it would be partly her fault. Because if she'd reported Phaeton as a stowaway right away, he'd never have been able to make all this trouble.

Pheme yanked open the door. And nearly ran into Athena, who was on her way into the office.

"Hi," said Athena.

"Hi," Pheme said back. Anxiously she wondered what Athena and Eros, not to mention Zeus, were going to think when they found out what she'd done. Sneaking Phaeton into MOA was probably a terrible offense.

Of course, that would be the least of her worries if the whole planet went kablooey!

Athena stepped around Pheme, went to the counter, and handed Ms. Hydra a sheet of papyrus. "Ms. Hecate in Spell-ology asked me to drop off this note."

Feeling like there was no time to lose, Pheme didn't wait around. She had to stop Phaeton before he started trouble! She dashed from the office so fast, she didn't even notice that Athena had begun to study her chariot drawing.

At the front doors of the Academy, Pheme kicked off her sandals. Then she grabbed the same pair of winged sandals she'd shucked off less than twenty minutes before, and headed out the door.

On the granite steps she paused to slip the sandals onto her feet. It was a good thing tomorrow was

Saturday. Even in winged sandals it would take a long time to reach Helios's golden palace. It stood at the eastern end of the Earth!

The wings at her heels began to flap. *Whoosh!* Soon she was skimming across the courtyard toward the trail that wound down to Earth. Even without stopping to rest, she'd be lucky if she managed to reach Helios's palace by sunrise tomorrow, she thought as she zipped away from the school. That's when the sun god's journey across the sky would begin anew in the east, as it did each day.

She rose in altitude, hoping to pick up speed. Traveling by chariot would've been faster than winged sandals, but she didn't have a chariot. Phaeton did, though. By now she was sure of it. A stolen one. And he also had a big head start.

Pegasus, Zeus's winged horse, was cavorting up ahead in the sky. As she passed him, she slowed briefly and gave him a quick pat. If only she could ride him, she'd soon catch up with Phaeton. Alas, Pegasus was not for loan and rarely allowed anyone but Zeus to ride him. Too bad she didn't have her *own* set of wings, like Eros did!

Pheme looked at the sky overhead. Shading her eyes from the glare, she watched Helios thunder westward. Crowned with the corona of the sun, he stood tall in the chariot, skillfully guiding his fiery horses. His purple robes billowed out behind him.

When the sun set this evening, it would mean that Helios had reached the land of the Hesperides, his westernmost destination. Night would fall, and he would descend into a golden cup that would carry him back to his palace in the east, where the sun would rise again tomorrow.

Who would get to the palace first—him or Phaeton?

Phaeton had said he would remain a mortal unless his family's mark of immortality were passed on to him. Rumor had it that Helios could send out solar flares to zap any mortals who displeased him. What if Helios wasn't pleased to see Phaeton? What a mess!

Whoo! Whoo! The cry of an owl drew Pheme's attention. Fixing her with its large blue-gray eyes, it glided down to fly alongside her. Astonished, Pheme tried to shoo it away.

But as it continued to keep pace with her, she turned suspicious. First of all, no owl had ever flown beside her before. Second, she'd never seen one with blue-gray eyes.

"Athena, is that you?" she asked. Like lots of other gods and goddesses, Athena could shape-shift. And everyone knew she usually took the form of an owl when she did. It was her favorite animal. Unfortunately, shape-shifting wasn't a talent Pheme possessed. Otherwise she could've changed herself into a peregrine falcon now and soared to the sun god's palace!

After brushing Pheme's shoulder with one of its wings, the owl then veered gracefully toward an orchard below. Sure that she was meant to follow, Pheme did. If this was Athena, she must want to talk, something she couldn't do while in owl form.

"Athena?" Pheme asked as she touched down.

"Whoo whoo else?" Athena asked as she shape-shifted back to her goddess form. "I saw your drawing in the office," she explained quickly. "Something's wrong, isn't it?"

Pheme nodded. "Phaeton's—" But that was as far as she could get before the familiar tickle came into her throat. She swallowed hard as the also familiar feeling of frustration washed over her.

"You were trying to tell us something about him at breakfast, weren't you?" said Athena.

Pheme nodded. She fixed the wings of her sandals so she could walk in them, then the girls headed onward on foot.

"So you figured out what that drawing meant?" Pheme asked.

"It took me a while," Athena told her, "but yes. You think Phaeton has taken Artemis's chariot, right? Dad's not very good at drawing either," she added. "By now I've gotten pretty good at deciphering the inartistic sketches he sometimes includes in his notes to me."

"Is that why you followed me? So you could dis my drawing skills? I've got to get to Helios's palace before—" But then Pheme stopped talking, because the tickle in her throat was back.

As she passed a fruit tree, she reached up to pick a couple of pears. She offered one to Athena, but Athena shook her head. Medusa had brought some ambrosia bars to share on their trip to see the Gray Ladies. But Pheme hadn't had anything to eat since then. She bit into the fruit and munched as they walked eastward.

"This is so annoying!" Pheme said between bites. "I can't tell you what I need to! Can you take your dumb spell off? It's important, I promise."

Looking distressed, Athena shook her head. "I'd remove it if I could. But I can't. There's nothing we can do but wait till the spell wears off on its own."

Pheme had been afraid that might be the case. "I need to go," she repeated, tossing away her half-eaten pear.

"I'm coming with you," Athena said. "Together we can travel faster."

"How?" asked Pheme. "You know I can't shape-shift."

"If you'll just let me cast a—"

"Oh, no," Pheme said, taking a couple of steps backward. "Not *another* spell!"

"Just a little one," Athena promised. "A very little one." Before Pheme could say another word, Athena uttered her spell:

You shall hitch a ride with me
As a teeny-tiny flea.

Instantly Pheme felt herself shrinking and growing lighter. And hoppier. *Boing! Boing!* Wow! Now she could hop over a thousand times higher than she was tall. She was a flea! A flea wearing a teeny-tiny chiton and winged sandals. The spell had shrunk them, too.

Ha! thought Pheme, recalling that Athena had called her spell *a very little one.* Few things were smaller than a flea!

In the meantime Athena had changed back into an

owl. *Boing!* Pheme hopped up onto her shoulder and nestled under one of her neck feathers. Then they were off.

They flew silently for several hours, unable to speak while in bird and bug form. If Pheme added in the hours she'd spent traveling with Medusa to the Gray Ladies' office that morning, this was the most time she'd ever spent whizzing through the air in a single day.

Eventually the sun began to set. Which meant that Helios had reached the land of the Hesperides. Soon his golden cup would carry him back to his palace.

Athena veered downward as the sky darkened. She was probably tired after hours spent skimming over forests and towns, across rivers and oceans, and above hills and mountains, Pheme figured. And Pheme would be glad for a rest herself. Because even though she wasn't

195

doing the flying, she *was* tired of being a flea. It felt, well, be*little*ing!

As soon as they touched down on Earth, they both regained their goddess forms. Pheme spotted a cave up ahead, and they took refuge inside. Both curled up to rest for an hour or two. At least that's how long they'd *intended* to sleep.

Kraak! Kraak!

"What was that?" Pheme sat up and looked at Athena. She was lying a few feet away, still dozing. They'd overslept. It was almost dawn!

Kraak! Kraak! Suddenly a creature with the body of a lion, and the front claws, head, and wings of an eagle appeared from deep inside the cave.

"Oh, no! A griffin!" whispered Pheme. It was headed their way. And it didn't look too happy to have visitors. No surprise, since cave-dwelling griffins were known to guard treasure. It was probably worried that the girls had come to steal whatever was hidden in the cave—gold, most likely.

"We don't want your treasure!" Pheme assured it as she inched over to nudge Athena.

Kraak! Kraak! An angry, disbelieving look shone in the griffin's ruby-red eyes. It flapped its enormous wings at them.

"Wake up, Athena!" Pheme shook the still-slumbering girl, who had somehow managed to sleep through the griffin's loud cries.

"Wah?" Athena said drowsily. Quickly Pheme slipped one of her own winged sandals—which had become normal size again after she'd regained her goddess form—onto Athena's bare foot. Then she slipped the other sandal back onto her own foot. As the laces twined around their ankles and the wings at their

197

heels began to flap, Pheme grabbed Athena's hand and tugged her toward the exit.

"Ye gods! Is that a griffin?" Athena shrieked just before their sandals whisked them out of the cave.

Kraaaak! The griffin flew at them, its wicked talons outstretched. Fortunately, it stopped at the entrance to the cave.

"Phew! That was close," said Pheme.

Now fully awake, Athena stared at her as they flew on in girl form, moving eastward.

Pheme braced herself, expecting Athena to condemn her for the poor judgment she'd shown in selecting that particular cave as a refuge. It wouldn't be fair, but that would be typical of the crummy way things were going in her life this week.

Instead Athena blurted out, "You just saved my life!" Of course, that wasn't exactly true. They were both immortal, and immortals couldn't die. But they still could've been hurt.

Athena wrapped her arm around Pheme's waist and gave her a quick hug. "Thanks."

The look in Athena's eyes as she smiled was one Pheme got so seldomly that it took her a few moments to puzzle it out. Finally she realized what it was. *Gratitude.*

11

Running Wild

JUST AS THE SKY BEGAN TO LIGHTEN ONLY moments before dawn, the girls reached Helios's gleaming golden palace at last. Three stories high with a gold-tiled roof and lots of gold columns, it was surrounded by an amazingly ornate golden gate. *At midday the palace must gleam as brightly as the sun itself!* thought Pheme.

"Look," Athena said, nudging Pheme with an elbow. "Artemis's deer!"

Sure enough, all four of the golden-antlered, milk-white deer were there in front of the magnificent palace. They were grazing on the wide lawn, and beyond them stood Artemis's chariot.

"It's lost a wheel," Athena noted as they touched down near the chariot. "Phaeton was probably driving it too recklessly. He could've benefited from Dad's chariot safety lecture." She bent to examine the damage.

Pheme looked around. "Where is that boy, anyway?" she muttered. They needed to find him right away!

A sudden shift of light drew the girls' eyes upward. The sky was turning pink. Dawn had come.

Helios's sun chariot rose from behind the palace gates, right on time. But something was horribly wrong!

"Why is it wobbling like that?" Athena asked.

A glance at the driver confirmed Pheme's worst fears. She pointed. "Because Phaeton's driving it. *Alone*. We got here too late!" The sun chariot rose higher, lurching this way and that. They didn't dare call out to him. He might lose control and crash!

"I'll go see if I can find the missing wheel for Artemis's chariot so we can catch him. You find Helios," suggested Athena.

With that, they separated, and Pheme ran to the palace gates. As she peered through the bars, Helios came racing out of the palace. His shining crown of sun rays slipped to one side as he ran, and the back of his purple robe flapped in the air behind him.

Cupping his hands around his mouth, he shouted to Phaeton, "Pull hard to your left, Son! You've got to make those horses respect you!" But Phaeton was already too far away to hear him.

Pheme rattled the gates, but they were locked. Her words puffed above her head as she shouted through the golden bars at Helios. "He'll never be able to handle those horses. You've got to stop him!"

Startled to see a visitor, Helios nevertheless waved an arm toward the gates, causing them to spring open. Barely glancing at Pheme, since his attention was on the chariot, he said, "There's no way to stop him. Unless you happen to have another sun chariot. Who are you, anyway?"

"I'm Pheme. I came here with Zeus's daughter Athena from Mount Olympus Academy," she said hurriedly. She pointed to Artemis's chariot. "Phaeton stole that, and . . ."

She paused, suddenly realizing that her throat felt

fine. And she wasn't making animal sounds. With the coming of dawn the twenty-four hours were over. The anti-gossip spell had ended. Now she could say whatever she wanted to again!

"No time to explain everything now," she told Helios. "Athena's trying to fix Artemis's chariot. We've got to act fast to stop Phaeton before he crashes into the Earth and everything goes up in flames!"

Helios shook his head mournfully. "Even if Athena does fix the chariot, it won't help. No mere deer-drawn chariot could ever catch my fiery steeds."

"Then we need to get a warning to Zeus!" Pheme exclaimed desperately. If Principal Zeus had seen and understood her drawing, he might already be on his way. But she couldn't count on that. She had to spread the news of the coming disaster far and wide and hope Zeus got wind of it before it was too late!

"Found it!" Athena shouted just then from the far side of the wide lawn. She was rolling the missing wheel across the grass. As soon as she reached the chariot, she began to wedge the wheel back into place. In the meantime Pheme whistled for Artemis's deer. She hitched them to the chariot as Helios helped Athena finish replacing the wheel.

"I'll take Artemis's chariot and try to get a message to Zeus," Pheme said when all was ready.

"Maybe I should go with you," Athena said anxiously. "What if the wheel falls off again and you need help getting it back on?"

Pheme shook her head. "I'll be fine." Her voice sounded more confident than she felt. Though she'd done okay in chariot safety classes, she'd never driven a chariot on a long journey like the one she now planned to undertake.

"All right, then," said Athena. "I'll stay and try to help Helios build a new chariot."

Pheme's knees shook as she climbed into the chariot and took up the reins. As Artemis's milk-white deer pulled the chariot into the sky, Pheme waved good-bye to Athena and Helios. If disaster came, she might never see them again!

Taking the most direct route toward Mount Olympus and the Academy, Pheme swooped low over every town and village she came to and shouted out her news. "Doomsday is coming! Helios's sun chariot is in danger of crashing! We must get word to Zeus! Run to the temples—pass the word to him!"

Now that she was no longer under Athena's spell, her words rang out loud and clear. And after puffing from her lips, they rose high in the air for all to see. The townspeople and villagers took up the call, spreading her message far and wide.

Despite never having flown a chariot outside the school grounds, Pheme had absorbed more lessons from all those chariot safety assemblies than she would've believed possible. Expertly she guided the deer over hills, through valleys, and across rivers, calling out her news to everyone she saw.

Meanwhile, the sun chariot continued to lurch crazily as it made its way across the sky above her. It was far larger than the one Pheme was driving, and its team of horses was much stronger than Artemis's deer. Looked like Phaeton was barely managing to hold on. And then suddenly he no longer could.

"Ye gods!" Pheme cried as she saw the horses wrench the reins free from his hands. He hung on for dear life as they began to run wild, slinging the sun chariot this way and that behind them.

As Pheme sailed onward, over the sea toward MOA, she watched Helios's horses gallop straight up to the very top of the sky. Then suddenly they plunged down, setting the tops of the mountains and hills surrounding Mount Olympus on fire!

Smoke billowed up around her. Pheme had never felt more terrified. Where was Zeus? Surely the warnings the mortals had sent from the temples must have reached him by now. If they hadn't, the sight of the fiery destruction would soon alert him. But by then it might be too late.

"Help!" she heard Phaeton cry out. He was mortal. He'd die if the sun chariot crashed. Of course, he wouldn't be the only one to perish if the Earth burned and the sun went out!

Still, what could *she* do to stop it from happening? She was no hero!

But then she remembered Athena's words and her look of gratitude as Pheme had whisked her from the griffin's cave. "You just saved my life!" she'd exclaimed. The memory gave Pheme courage.

She watched as Helios's horses soared high into the air again. She knew it was only a matter of seconds before they went into another dive. When they did, she would be ready.

As the horses began to plunge toward another hill, Pheme spurred Artemis's deer toward it. "Bail out as you near the ground," she shouted to Phaeton. "Then roll downhill. I'll be waiting!"

Even though she'd shouted as loud as she could, there was no way he would hear her words from so far away. But maybe he would see them. Her puffed words floated higher than ever before—large and clearly visible above the smoke and fire.

Seconds later there was a burst of flame among the hills as the golden horses touched down again. Then all was obscured in a dense curtain of smoke.

Pheme landed at the bottom of the burning hill to wait, hoping against hope that Phaeton had seen her message, that he had been able to jump clear of the chariot and the fire and would soon appear before her eyes.

As the horses broke free of the smoke and began to climb again, she strained to see if the foolish boy was still in the sun god's chariot. But before the chariot could rise from the smoke, a winged figure burst through the clouds above her.

It was Zeus! Riding on Pegasus! And he was holding an enormous, sizzling thunderbolt. Speechless with horror, she saw him draw back his arm and hurl the bolt with all his might.

Ka-BOOM! It struck Helios's sun chariot and blew it to smithereens. As the pieces fell to Earth, the team of fiery horses bolted safely away.

And except for the flames in the hills, the entire world went dark.

12

A New Dawn

GRADUALLY PHEME WAS ABLE TO MAKE OUT Phaeton's figure stumbling in the surrounding darkness as fires still raged behind him. She sagged against the side of Artemis's chariot in relief. He wasn't dead. At least something had gone right!

Cradling his right arm in his left one, he climbed up beside her in Artemis's chariot. "Are you okay?"

she asked, peering at him through the dimness.

"I think so," he said. "Just a few scrapes and burns. Nothing major. But where'd the sun go?"

Now that she knew he wasn't badly hurt, anger rose up inside her. "It was destroyed, obviously!" she scolded. "Not to mention that Earth and Mount Olympus almost got burned up. The fires still rage even now. How could you be so totally stupid?"

Phaeton hung his head. "I'm sorry."

She scowled. No apology would ever be enough for what he'd done. What if the sun never returned? She'd taken Science-ology. She knew nothing could live without sunlight. Not for long anyway.

"Hey, something's happening," Phaeton said, looking around. "I can see the grass again. And the mountains. You're clearer now too."

"The sky!" Pheme whispered in awe. "It's getting lighter."

Just then something soared from the clouds and smoke to ride high in the sky. A brand-new sun chariot! With Helios holding its reins. Under his firm hand the four fiery steeds were calm again, crossing the eastern-most heavens in their usual way.

Phaeton gaped at the sight. "Who made—"

"Athena," said Pheme. "She's amazing with chariots. With her skill and magic, looks like she and Helios created a whole new one in the nick of time!"

"But the horses," Phaeton sputtered in confusion.

"They must've raced back to the palace stables after they were freed from the sun chariot that was destroyed."

Crack! They both ducked low in Artemis's chariot as a lightning bolt suddenly speared across the sky. And then another bolt, and another. Dark clouds formed in the distance.

"Look," Phaeton said, pointing toward the hills. "It's raining!"

"Zeus," Pheme breathed. "He's started a storm to put out the fires around Olympus."

"So no harm done after all," said Phaeton, smiling broadly. "It was just a temporary blackout. Like an eclipse! Now that it's light, we can go back to MOA." He took up the chariot's reins.

Pheme let out a huge huff of annoyance. She couldn't believe he was taking this almost-disaster so lightly! Growing brisk, she said, "Yes, time to head for MOA again. But *I'll* do the driving."

Phaeton gave up the reins without protest. Maybe deep down he really did understand that his actions had nearly brought about the end of the world.

As Artemis's deer-drawn chariot took them into the

sky again, Pheme considered heading back to Helios's palace to pick up Athena. But they were pretty close to MOA by now. She decided to check there first to see if Athena had shape-shifted to fly back to the Academy. Or if her dad had taken her there.

On the flight home Pheme called out to the mortals below, spreading the word that disaster had been averted and everything was going to be all right. There would be no way to let Helios know that Phaeton was okay until dawn, when he returned to the palace.

Phaeton was quiet during their journey, and she didn't press him with questions. Not that she didn't have any. She certainly did. But she was also still mad at him. She didn't want to hear any excuses he might offer for his behavior.

Students were all over the courtyard when their chariot—that is, *Artemis's* chariot—touched down. Pheme wondered how much they knew. They might've seen the fires. And they surely would've noticed the sun's disappearance for several minutes during daylight hours, but did they know what had caused these things?

She could tell everyone, she thought as she and Phaeton jumped down from the chariot. She *wanted* to tell everyone. But when she glanced at Phaeton and noted his slumped shoulders and the look of shame on his face, she hesitated. "When in doubt, don't shout it out," she remembered the tall Gray Lady advising.

While Pheme was thinking this over, she and Phaeton silently unhooked the deer from the chariot. Breaking through a knot of students, Artemis ran up to them. "Delta, Hypatia, Eudora, Callista," she cried, hugging each deer in turn. "I was afraid I'd never see you again!"

After cooing over her deer, she suddenly turned

on Pheme. "How dare you borrow my chariot without asking!" Her face was red with fury.

Before Pheme could even open her mouth, Phaeton came to her defense. "*I* took it," he said. "Pheme only flew it back after she rescued me. I—"

Whoo! Whoo! The hoot of a large brown owl interrupted him. It swooped down toward them and landed on the edge of the chariot.

Athena! Pheme thought happily. The owl's wings became arms, and its feathers turned to glittering skin as Athena shape-shifted back to her goddess form.

"I'm so glad you and Phaeton are okay," Athena told her, hopping down from the chariot.

"Tell me about it! I was triple-mega-happy when I saw Helios flying that new sun chariot," said Pheme.

Athena laughed. "Helios and I probably set a record for the fastest chariot ever built."

As the two girls hugged each other, students began to gather around them, eager for news of the morning's events.

Athena quickly turned toward Artemis. "Yesterday at breakfast Pheme noticed your chariot was missing. And she suspected Phaeton had taken it. She did try to tell us, but of course she couldn't since she was under my anti-gossiping spell."

Pheme glanced at the crowd of students listening in. Most of them knew she'd taken part in a *challenge* yesterday, but they didn't know why she'd agreed to it. She hoped that her diary-snooping secret would remain safe among those who did know.

Artemis gave the two girls a puzzled look. "But my chariot was sitting at the side of the Academy when Apollo and I left for our archery competition yesterday after lunch. I know because just before we started down the trail to Earth, I realized I'd forgotten to feed my deer and came back to do it."

"That first time I only borrowed it for a little while to practice," Phaeton admitted, confirming what Pheme had suspected. "I didn't start out for my dad's palace until after lunch—after I saw you feed the deer and leave." He lowered his head. "I'm sorry."

Artemis frowned. "Well, you should be!" With a disgusted sound she turned away from him to fawn over her deer some more and to check her chariot for damage.

"Listen up, everyone," Athena called to the crowd. "You may not know this, but Pheme is a hero! She saved me from an angry griffin, rescued Phaeton—"

"AND HELPED SAVE THE WORLD FROM DESTRUCTION!" a voice from above boomed out. Zeus!

In mere seconds he and Pegasus settled down to

the courtyard's marble tiles. After springing from the winged horse's back, Zeus strode right up to Pheme.

"Ms. Hydra gave me your message," he said, pulling her now crumpled-up drawing from his tunic pocket. "This is just the kind of drawing I like," he said. "Simple. Direct. No unnecessary lines." His blue eyes twinkled. "I understood it right away."

He did? Pheme was amazed. "Well, you know what they say."

Zeus cocked his head. "What's that?"

Pheme grinned. "A doodle is worth a thousand words!"

Zeus threw back his head, and his laughter boomed out across the Academy grounds. Then, catching sight of Phaeton, he stopped midchortle. "You there!" he called out in a stern voice. "To my office, boy!"

Then he nodded to Pheme. "And you. Stop by my

office in a half hour." Glancing at Athena, he added, "You come with her, Theeny."

Phaeton looked petrified as he trailed after Principal Zeus. Even though she was still mad at that boy, Pheme couldn't help feeling sorry for him. She knew what it was like to fear the principal's wrath. And what Phaeton had done was way more potentially dangerous than anything she'd ever done. He was definitely in for it.

"Hooray for Pheme!" someone in the crowd yelled. Was that Eros's voice? She didn't see him, but . . . "Way to go!" someone else shouted. Soon everyone was cheering for her. In their eyes she saw a new respect for her because of what she'd done.

She could hardly believe it. She'd never gotten this much attention before. Not *positive* attention, anyway. It was the same kind of respect she hoped the reporter job would bring her. If she got it.

And then it hit her. Now—while Zeus and everyone else was so happy with her—would be the perfect time to ask him to write that letter of recommendation! When they went to his office, she was going to ask him for sure.

Athena gave her a thumbs-up as the cheering died down. "Meet you in Dad's office in a few," she said as Heracles came up to talk to her.

Pheme nodded, then looked around for Eros. She was pretty sure he'd been the one to start the cheers. And she wanted to thank him for suggesting she use her doodles to communicate while under Athena's spell.

Other students began crowding around her. "I can't believe you went to Helios's palace."

"What was Phaeton up to?"

"What was the trip like?"

"Hey, let the girl eat first," said a voice. Eros! He came

223

flying across the courtyard, his golden wings gently flapping. The crowd scattered as he touched down next to her. Those wings of his were so awesome. Not to mention fast.

With a flourish he handed her something wrapped in a sheet of papyrus. "A hero sandwich for a hero."

"Food!" said Pheme, grinning. She took the foot-long sandwich he held out to her and unwrapped it. "Thanks. I'm absolutely famished!"

They sat on a nearby bench, and between bites of sandwich she told him all about the long journey with Athena.

His eyes widened when he heard about the griffin. "Close call."

She nodded. "It usually takes me a while to get going when I first wake up. But not *that* time. Athena and I were out of that cave lickety-split!"

Eros laughed, and so did she. "Well, I'm glad you're okay." He shifted, and his wings fluttered.

"You're so lucky to have those," she said, nudging one of his wings with the side of her arm. "If I'd had some of my own, I could've flown after Phaeton yesterday morning when I first saw him in Artemis's chariot."

Eros nodded. "Wings are amazing," he agreed. "They let you fly high and travel fast."

Just imagine! With wings she could spread news faster and farther than ever, thought Pheme. She might even be able to eavesdrop on people from overhead. How cool would that be? She glanced wistfully at Eros's wings again.

He noticed the direction of her gaze. "And that's another good thing about my wings," he said with a grin. "They attract the attention of girls."

Pheme straightened, blushing.

"Plus, they make a nice breeze when it's hot," Eros added. "And I can shoo away enemies with them. Small ones at least."

Pheme laughed. "Wings are definitely awesome."

"Yes, but *you're* awesome even without them," he told her earnestly. Then, as if he'd just realized what he'd said, his apple-red cheeks grew even redder.

"Thanks." Pheme smiled at him, and Eros smiled back. He had the cutest dimples, she thought. A warm feeling spread through her. It was sort of like the feeling she got from delivering an especially juicy piece of gossip. Only better. Sweeter.

"So what's the deal with you and Phaeton, anyway?" Eros asked out of the blue.

"The deal?" Having finished her sandwich, Pheme balled up the papyrus wrapping it had come in. Then she recalled the bargain she and Phaeton had made when she'd enrolled him at MOA. "Oh, yeah we did have a deal, but—"

Eros's feathers ruffled in annoyance as he interrupted her. "That guy's kind of bad news, don't you think? He's a chariot thief, for one thing. And he almost burned down the world! You know, I wonder if Zeus really invited him to MOA. Maybe he just sneaked in on his own."

Pheme's hand flew to her throat. "Huh?" she asked nervously. As far as she knew, no one had guessed that Phaeton had come here as a stowaway, or that she was the one who'd enrolled him. But if Eros was wondering, others would be too. Like Zeus. Zeus could be absent-minded, though. Maybe he wouldn't realize he hadn't actually invited Phaeton to attend MOA.

"I wonder if he really even *is* Helios's son," Eros went on.

"He is," Pheme said. "Helios said so." She wondered

227

if Eros was angry at Phaeton because of the tragedy he'd almost caused, or— Wait! Was it possible he was jealous?

"If you think I'm crushing on him—or vice versa—you're wrong," she told him.

He stared at her. "Then I'm confused," he told her. "What's your connection with him? Why did you go after him?"

She guessed she'd better explain all, and tell him the truth about why she'd accepted Athena's challenge. Before he found out from someone else. But what would he think when he knew?

"Accept your imperfections," Pheme remembered the small Gray Lady saying. Pheme knew she wasn't perfect. If Eros really did like her—*like* like her, that is—then he'd accept her imperfections too. If he couldn't, then . . .

228

"If you really want to know," said Pheme, "I'll tell you everything."

"Yeah, I do," said Eros. He settled back on the bench to listen.

Pheme began with the snooping that turned her hands red, and then told him about meeting Phaeton shortly afterward as a stowaway on Hermes' chariot. And how he'd claimed his father was a god but wouldn't tell her his name until she helped him get into MOA.

"Wait a second," Eros said. "Go back to the red hands. Did Athena find out about your snooping? Was that the reason for the no-gossip spell?"

"Yes," Pheme admitted.

"Well, I still think it was wrong of her to put you through that," said Eros. "Gossip is as essential as . . . as *love*!" he exclaimed. "It's true that both can cause trouble and pain at times. But without gossip, any news—good *or* bad—might not get shared at all."

Pheme smiled. "And without love no one would ever find the girl or boy of their dreams."

He beamed at her. "Exactly!"

It was obvious that she needn't have worried about Eros judging her. What a relief! *If he is crushing on me,* she thought, *I kind of like it.*

Just then Athena waved to her from across the courtyard. "Time to go see Dad," she called out.

"Okay," Pheme called back. She got up from the bench. "Thanks for listening," she told Eros.

"Sure," he replied. He stood up, hands in his pockets. "Um, I'll take you flying sometime if you want to see how my wings work."

"Really?" Pheme asked, eyeing his soft golden feathers. If they went, would she need to wear a pair of winged sandals since she couldn't fly on her own? Or maybe they would just hold hands. . . .

"Pheme!" Athena called again.

"Coming!" Pheme called back.

"Later, then," Eros told her. "And good luck with that *Teen Scrollazine* job." His wings fluttered together to form an 'X' behind him. "Wings crossed that you get it."

"Thanks." She grinned, pleased that he'd remembered about that. She turned to go. "Later," she called over her shoulder to him as she raced to catch up with Athena. Then the two girls rushed up the granite steps to the principal's office.

13

Wing Things

Go RIGHT IN. HE'S EXPECTING YOU," MS. HYDRA told Pheme and Athena as they entered the outer office.

The girls passed the assistant's desk, then hesitated outside Zeus's open door. Phaeton had his back to them as he stood before the principal's massive desk.

Waving a sheet of papyrus clutched in his fist, Zeus roared at the boy, "And just who gave you permission to attend Mount Olympus Academy? Because *I* didn't. I'm pretty sure I'd remember if I had!"

Pheme gulped. *Uh-oh.* If she wasn't mistaken, that sheet of papyrus Zeus was waving around was the enrollment form she'd filled out on Phaeton's behalf. She'd hoped that the question of how Phaeton had come to be enrolled at MOA would just go away on its own. Apparently that wasn't going to happen.

She held her breath, waiting to see if Phaeton would rat her out. What would Zeus do once he knew? Order her to leave the Academy and never return? And he'd been so pleased with her only minutes earlier!

Before Phaeton could respond, Zeus glanced up and saw the girls. Dropping the papyrus form on his desk, he motioned to a couple of chairs. "Sit! I'll be finished here in a minute."

Both chairs bore scorch marks, Pheme noticed.

Probably singed by random bolts of electricity he'd zapped toward other students who'd been seated before him at one time or another.

As the girls sat, the principal's gaze swung back to Phaeton again. "WELL?" he boomed.

Phaeton darted a look at Pheme over one shoulder. Then he straightened determinedly and faced Zeus. "I enrolled myself," he fibbed.

Zeus's eyebrows shot up. "WHAT? HOW?"

"I . . . um . . . I filled out that form and—"

"Stop!" said Pheme, jumping up. There was a moment of startled silence as everyone turned to look at her. No one was more surprised at her outburst than she was. However, despite what Phaeton had done, she couldn't let him take the rap for something he *hadn't* done.

She sank back into her chair and took a deep breath

for courage. "*I* enrolled him," she admitted. "I erased an old form I found, filled it in, and dropped it in a stack of papers on Ms. Hydra's desk when her heads weren't looking."

"Sorry, Ms. Hydra," she called back over her shoulder when she noticed the administrative assistant's grumpy green head lurking in the doorway.

"Humph," groused the head, withdrawing.

Her confession meant that she could kiss the *Teen Scrollazine* job good-bye, Pheme knew. No way would she get a good recommendation from Zeus after this. And even if he didn't send her packing for home immediately, she'd undoubtedly lose her job with Ms. Hydra in the front office and probably her floor monitor job too.

Zeus's red eyebrows scrunched up, and he stared at Pheme with a look of confusion. "But why did you do it?"

"Because it was the only way Phaeton would agree to tell me who his dad was," she told Zeus. She paused to send Phaeton an apologetic glance, then continued. "I was looking for a big story, and I—I just *had* to know. You see, I—" But just as she was going to explain about the recommendation she'd hoped to get from him, Athena cut her off.

"She *is* the goddess of gossip and rumor, Dad," she said in Pheme's defense. "So maybe you could cut her some slack?"

Pheme shot her a grateful look. She doubted he'd really let the enrollment form issue slide, but it was nice of Athena to try.

Zeus drummed his fingers on the desktop, sending sparks flying. "All right," he said after a moment. "I'll ignore the enrollment issue. For now."

Whoa! thought Pheme. He was taking this revelation much better than she'd expected. But maybe it was only because what she'd done paled in comparison to Phaeton's actions.

Zeus's intense blue eyes had fastened on Phaeton again. "It's true that Helios is your father," he said. "But he was a softhearted fool to let you drive his chariot."

Pheme's head jerked back in surprise. Helios had *intentionally* let Phaeton drive his chariot? This was news. Until that moment she'd assumed that Phaeton had helped himself to it the same way he'd "borrowed" Artemis's chariot. Well, if Helios had *let* Phaeton take it, then the sun god was more than softhearted. He was soft*headed*, too!

"It wasn't his fault," Phaeton protested. "I kind of tricked him. Only, I didn't know how hard it would be to control those horses." He hesitated a moment, then added, "But it was thrilling all the same. I mean, I'm sorry I almost destroyed the world." Raising his chin, Phaeton added stubbornly, "But I'm not sorry I drove my dad's chariot."

"WHAT?" Zeus slammed his fist on his desk, and more sparks shot out.

"Look." Phaeton held up his arm so that Zeus and the girls could see it. Where the sun fire had singed him, a small patch of his skin in the shape of a sun with rays shooting out was glistening. And the glow was spreading. "It's my family's special mark. I'm shimmering now, like a real godboy," he said proudly. "Which I am."

A variety of expressions, from anger to amusement, flitted across Zeus's face at the same time. "You young immortals!" he muttered finally, running his fingers through his hair. "So anxious to try things before you're old enough to handle them!"

Pheme wondered if he knew that from experience.

She started to ask, but Phaeton spoke before she could.

"So will you send me home now?" he asked.

Zeus sat back on his throne and nodded. "You've broken more rules than I can count. Hermes will take you home after you leave my office." Then he added gruffly, "If you can stay out of trouble, I *might* invite you to attend MOA next year."

Phaeton smiled, looking flabbergasted. Then he pumped a shimmery fist in the air. "Woo-hoo! Thank you, thank you, thank you, Principal Zeus. And did I mention thank you? I'll try to be worthy of an invitation. I'll stick it out at Ima Luzer. I promise!"

"'I'm a Loser'?" Zeus echoed.

"The name of his school," Pheme informed him.

"Godsamighty," said Zeus shaking his head. "Well, see that you take a chariot safety course sometime this year. Before you try driving any chariots again."

"Deal!" said Phaeton.

"Theeny," Zeus said to Athena, "escort Phaeton to the courtyard. Hermes should be waiting for him there. I want to talk to Pheme for a few minutes alone."

For about the millionth time that day, Pheme found herself practically paralyzed with fear. Still she managed to smile bravely at Phaeton and Athena as they made their way toward the office door together.

She wondered if Principal Zeus knew about the anti-gossip spell she'd been under yesterday. If he started asking questions, she might have to tell him about it. That would lead to revealing that she'd snooped in the girls' dorm and read Athena's diaryscroll. On top of everything else, that would seal her doom for sure.

However, it also might make him mad at Athena for putting a spell on her that delayed her ability to report important news about Phaeton. Pheme didn't want to create problems for Athena. She hoped she wouldn't have to tell. . . .

Lost in her thoughts, she jumped when Zeus cleared his throat to get her attention. "AHEM!" Steepling his hands beneath his red-bearded chin, he leaned his elbows on the desktop and gave her a long, appraising look.

Uh-oh, thought Pheme. *Here comes trouble.* But he didn't return to the subject of forged enrollment forms or ask about spells or doodles. Instead he said, "Do you know how many messages I got this morning from temples, oracles, and mortals telling me that doomsday was coming and Helios's chariot was about to crash?"

Pheme shrugged, having no clue. "Twenty?" she guessed.

"HA!" Zeus exclaimed. "More like a *thousand*!"

"Wow," said Pheme. She'd had no idea her message

had spread so effectively. "I'm glad," she told him earnestly.

"Well, I just wanted you to realize how much I depend on you to keep me informed about the goings-on around here," he said. He started to rise, as if preparing to end their meeting.

"You know, it's hard being the goddess of gossip sometimes," she blurted. "I worry about missing things that might later turn out to be important. So sometimes I go overboard in what I collect and pass on."

Zeus sank back onto his throne. He regarded her thoughtfully. "As you know, the safety of MOA students and staff and the mortals on Earth is my biggest concern. You only need to report to me about things relating to that." He began to rise again to dismiss her.

"Yes, but it's not always easy for me to know which things might be a safety concern," Pheme dared to say.

Zeus sat again as she went on. "And sometimes I get things wrong—like with Freya's necklace." Oops! Why had she brought *that* up? She rushed on.

"The thing is, I never know if the stuff I do pass on to you will help—or just create problems," she confided. "But I'll go crazy if I have to second-guess every single bit of gossip."

Zeus nodded. "Yes, I think I understand."

He did?

Then Zeus said something that made her want to throw her arms around him and give him a hug. "You are who you are, Pheme," he told her. "Some people will blame you for what you do. Others will praise you. It's the same for me in my job as King of the Gods and Ruler of the Heavens. But don't ever forget that you're import- ant to this school. And as long as you're doing the best job you can, that's good enough for me."

Pheme could hardly believe her ears. Despite his anger over the Freya incident, Zeus seemed to accept that she would sometimes make mistakes. Best of all, he wasn't planning to kick her out of MOA as she'd feared!

"Um, I'm sorry about faking that enrollment form for Phaeton," she felt honor-bound to add.

One of Zeus's bushy red eyebrows lifted. "Yes, that wasn't your best idea. Still, he was pretty determined. Probably would've gone to see Helios regardless. At least this way you were able to find out what he was up to and get a warning to me in time to avert disaster."

"True—I hadn't thought of that!"

Zeus rose from his throne again and began to pace the floor. Since his office was a mess as usual, he trampled a few things underfoot. *Crunch!* went a Cyclops-opoly game piece. *Squish!* went an empty bottle of Zeus Juice. He hardly noticed.

"In fact, today's near-disaster was too close for comfort," he said, as if thinking out loud. "You should be able to travel faster in emergencies."

He stopped suddenly, one foot atop a smushed model of a temple, looking pleased with himself. "I just got a brilliant idea—not that I ever have any other kind, of course! I've decided I'll give you a chariot of your own. Or the ability to shape-shift."

"Wow!" Pheme considered the ideas, thrilled by them. She had come to his office expecting to be punished, and now he was offering her a gift! She'd enjoyed driving Artemis's chariot, and being able to shape-shift would be fantastic. But she knew what she'd rather have.

"Wings!" she told Zeus. "Could I have wings instead? Please?"

"Hmm," he said. "That's not a bad idea, even if I *didn't* think of it first! What kind?"

"Cute small girly ones with glitter," she told him quickly. "And make them orange. It's my favorite color," she told him.

"Really?" he said, grinning. "I'd never have guessed."

She glanced down at her orange chiton, then grinned back at him. Zeus didn't always have the best taste in the world, so she'd tried to be as specific as possible. She didn't want to end up with drab wings. Or wings that were so gigantic and unwieldy that she wouldn't be able to walk down the hall without knocking people over.

"All righty, then!" Zeus said enthusiastically. As she stood before him, he cast a spell.

"Small orange wings spring forth and flitter."

He knitted his forehead, as if trying to remember something, then added,

"Oh! And don't forget lots of sparkly glitter."

Then he spun her around. She heard the crackle of sparks flying from his fingers and felt a tickling sensation between her shoulder blades. Wings began to sprout there, pushing through the back of her chiton! She turned her head over her shoulder and was beside herself with joy when she saw them for the first time. Her very own wings!

"They're perfect," she breathed in awe. And they were. They were many iridescent shades of orange and looked kind of like butterfly wings, only they were about a foot and a half from top tip to bottom tip.

Zeus smiled. "Use them wisely," he told her. "And, again, good job today! Dismissed."

Job! Wait! That reminded her. Before he could shoo her off, Pheme grabbed her chance. "There's something

I've been wanting to ask you," she said, whipping around to face him. Then she told him all about her job application to *Teen Scrollazine* and the letter of recommendation she needed from him.

"No problem," he said. He bent over his desk, grabbed a piece of papyrus, and scribbled a letter straightaway.

Having perfected the art of reading upside down—a useful skill for a goddess of gossip—Pheme was able to read as Zeus wrote:

To Whom It May Concern,

I, Zeus—principal of Mount Olympus Academy as well as King of the Gods and Ruler of the

Heavens—hereby order you to hire
Pheme.

Yours in Thunder,

Zeus

Well, that was short and sweet, thought Pheme as Zeus pressed his official seal—a blazing gold *Z* shaped like a thunderbolt—onto the letter. Not quite the glowing recommendation she'd hoped for, but it should do the trick. After all, who would go against the wishes of the King of the Gods!

As Pheme hurried with her precious letter out the door and down the hall, she flapped her wings just a little. She was thrilled when she rose a few inches in the air.

"No flying in the halls," a teacher coming from the other direction called out.

"Sorry," Pheme called back, though she wasn't. Not really. But she quickly touched down again and folded her new wings closed. She couldn't wait to show them off. To Eros. And Athena. And everyone!

Would Eros go with her the first time she tried out her wings for real and give her some tips? She could hardly wait to ask him!

Epilogue

One week later

PHEME WAS ADMIRING HER NEW WINGS IN THE mirror by her desk after school one afternoon when her window began to rattle noisily. It blew open. Her beaded curtain shook as a glittery breeze rushed through it, carrying a rolled-up piece of papyrus. "Message from *Teen Scrollazine*," the breeze howled.

Giving a little squeal, Pheme fluttered over to the window and caught the scroll letter as it dropped toward the floor. "Thanks for the delivery!" she called to the breeze as it whooshed away.

Her wings trembled with excitement as she untied the silver ribbon from around the papyrus, unrolled the scroll letter, and began to read:

Dear Pheme,

Thank you for your recent application for the position of student staff reporter at Teen Scrollazine. We received many fine applications for this position, and yours was one of them. We regret to inform you, however, that your application was not selected and the position has now been filled.

Pheme gasped. What? *Regret to inform you? Not selected? Position filled?* That couldn't be right. She must have misread! She scanned the last line again, but the words were still the same.

There was more to the letter, but Pheme stopped reading. Her heart sank, her wings drooped, and her eyes blurred with tears. How could this have happened? She'd been so sure she'd be hired!

After sinking into her desk chair, she dropped the letterscroll onto her desk. It rolled off the edge and onto the floor. As she bent to pick it up, her eyes fell on the word "heroic." That sounded a little better.

She sat again and finished the lines she hadn't bothered to read before:

WE'RE AWARE OF THE HEROIC

PART YOU PLAYED RECENTLY IN

AVERTING DISASTER ON EARTH AND
MOUNT OLYMPUS, AND WISH TO
CONGRATULATE YOU.

That's nice, she thought. But it didn't make up for not getting the job. Still, she read on:

WE'D ALSO LIKE YOU TO KNOW
THAT WE'RE CREATING A BRAND-NEW
POSITION AT TEEN SCROLLAZINE,
AND ARE WONDERING IF YOU'D BE
INTERESTED.

Huh? Pheme's heart began to beat faster.

THIS WOULD BE A WEEKLY GOSSIP
COLUMN. TOPICS OF YOUR CHOICE. AND

ILLUSTRATED WITH THOSE CLEVER
DOODLES OF YOURS. PLEASE WRITE US
AT YOUR EARLIEST CONVENIENCE. AND
LET US KNOW YOUR THOUGHTS. WE'D
BE HONORED TO HAVE THE GODDESS OF
GOSSIP AS A PART OF OUR ILLUSTRIOUS
STAFF!

SINCERELY,

MR. HESIOD, EDITOR IN CHIEF
TEEN SCROLLAZINE

"Woo-hoo!" yelled Pheme, jumping around the room. Gossip columnist was an even better job than student staff reporter, in her humble opinion. A perfectly *respectable* job she'd have fun doing.

255

Right then and there she dashed off a reply accepting the new position. She added a few doodles, too, since the editor had seemed to like the ones she'd drawn in the margins of her application.

Then she wrote a second letterscroll telling her family all about her new job. When they'd heard about her role in saving the world from destruction, her parents had written to tell her how very proud they were.

And her twelve siblings had decorated their letter with doodles too—of her driving Artemis's chariot and rescuing Phaeton. At least she *thought* that's what the doodles showed. It seemed that artistic talent didn't run in her family. But love did, she thought. Even if she was sometimes slow to see it.

Pheme rolled up both letterscrolls and tied them with ribbons. She called up a magic breeze to deliver her messages.

After the breeze took them away, she did something she'd never done before. She sank back into her chair, reread the last paragraphs of the *Teen Scrollazine* letter again, and *quietly* savored her triumph. All by herself!

For about two seconds, that is.

Then, springing from her chair, she raced out of her room. As she flew down the hall, down the stairs, into the cafeteria, and through the MOA courtyard, she shouted out her wonderful news for all to hear.

"Guess what, everybody? I'm going to be the new gossip columnist for *Teen Scrollazine*!" Her words rose in big joyful cloud-letters to hover in the air everywhere she went.

Don't miss the next adventure in
the Goddess Girls series!

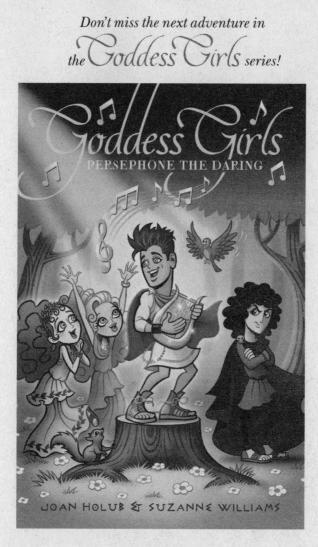

Coming soon!

Goddess Girls